Kaisa's Folly
By Jen Williams

November 2006

Mange takk, Dave Wyndorf, Tomas Haugen and Andrea Meyer Haugen! And most of all, thank you, Dave Brock-without whom Eroc would have never taken his fateful first flights on Blackwyrd.

Styrkar stared at the smoldering ruins of the village below and wept silently. He embraced in his young arms the one thing he was able to save-his father's great sword. In his pocket was a scorched metal flask that held the ashes-at least some of the ashes-of his parents. His head was swimming in thought-his mother's bloodied face, the riders with torches setting fire to the village, his father overwhelmed by the invaders and his subsequent beheading, the guilt of being the sole survivor of the attack.

As the sun sank behind the mountains, he finally ascended the ridge, penniless and starving, in hopes of fulfilling the oath he swore to his mother to hunt down and kill the riders, as well as their master, the dread king Aethelwulf.

Word of the invasion, as well as of other atrocities throughout the neighboring realm, reached the golden city of Aardsberg. The mighty hero of the North Arnkell had been murdered and his head was now impaled on a steel shaft upon the battlements of Aethelwulf's castle, along with the heads and bodies of others who had served King Hothgar, who had been said to have fled the invasion for a place yet unknown. Despite the persecutions and waves of refugees, Aardsberg closed its gates, refusing asylum. Still, Styrkar found his way into the great city. He had joined a mass of refuges heading for Aarsberg from the northern tribes and cities. When the city's militia refused entry, he crept off, remembering what Arnkell had told him about cities having escape tunnels so that rulers could flee from a siege that was not tilting in their favor.

On a steep, craggy slope, he found a crude trail hewn in the black rocks and scrambled up it. In a forgotten cemetery of old rotting wood paupers' graves was a mausoleum of grey stained marble and within, Styrkar found a hidden tunnel. He clawed along in the darkness, drips from unseen springs echoing around him softly, until he emerged under a rust encrusted iron grate through which he made out dim light above. Pushing it aside, he found himself in catacombs beneath the palace, where the royal family of Aardsberg had interred their dead.

It did not take him long to find his way out by a servants' entrance and into the population of Aardsberg, where he would live like a beggar, albeit a secretly and heavily armed beggar, for the next two years.

Aardsberg did not lend itself well to the poor, in both image and policy. It had wide streets paved in marble of all kinds and plazas full of exotic trees and shiny bronze fountains kept polished by slaves bought from islands Styrkar had never even heard of and alabaster statues of the greatest military heroes and rulers. The buildings were towering, capped with gleaming, colorful domes. The people of Aardsberg went to the bustling marketplaces in garish costume and beggars were often captured and thrown into oubliettes until the merchants would leave before the Witching Season, which brought storms of frightful winds and inundating rains, in order to make it home safely. In the shadows of these buildings and hiding in the alleys lurked the strange, silent boy with the mysterious bundle tied to his back.

The threat of Aethelwulf would not stay away for long, however, and a call for new students for the military academy went out. Among the men and boys answering the call was the adolescent Styrkar. At first, the recruiters scoffed and laughed at the idea of a stuttering beggar seeking to take up arms along side noblemen and gentry. Their ridiculing and guffaws caused Styrkar to leave in a blind fury, but he was followed out by a dark-haired female paladin, who had walked in on the incident.

He walked faster than her, so she hastily signaled a passing guard to stop him. Upon

approaching the boy, she could see he had the features of the famously brave Northern

Horsemen, whose greatest hero had been Arnkell Darkhorse. His eyes were a fiery,

defiant blue, but with a great sadness behind them, his blonde hair flowed in the light

breeze and he towered over her, even though he was no older than fifteen. She introduced

herself as Kaisa, a paladin of the Order of the Blue Tyger, and asked him who he might

be. He told her he was Styrkar, Son of Arnkell and he unbundled the great sword and

presented it to her as proof of his identity.

She took the warm, glowing blade into her hands and examined it with the awe of a

child. It was heavy and bore upon its pommel and hilt the symbols of Arnkell and the

Northern Horsemen tribes. It had been those legends of Arnkell and his heroism that

inspired her to seek out the life of a paladin, and now she beheld the weapon of those

sagas.

Her gaze then turned to the grimy, gangly boy that stood before her and realized that the

gods had brought Arnkell's son to her. He was the one who sought vengeance for the

death of his father and it would be him that she would put her faith in to save Aardsberg.

The gods had made her the one to train him to reach that destiny.

She took Styrkar back to the academy with her, ordering the recruiters to sign him in and

sponsoring his training, for she believed he was the only hope against Aethelwulf.

Reluctantly, they complied, nicknaming the boy "Styrkar, Kaisa's Folly".

But Styrkar was everything but a folly. So strong was his desire for vengeance and to

fulfill his oath to his mother that he worked hard to become a great warrior. Surprisingly,

he did not choose his father's cherished blade as his own, but rather a curious pair of weapons-a battle axe and a long sword. This piqued Kaisa's curiosity and she one day, after a rather rough exercise session, asked the boy why he did not choose the great sword as his weapon. He replied that his decision was because he was not his father. In secret, he was not eager to use his father's sword because he feared deeply he could never live up to Arnkell's reputation and would prove unworthy of it. He did, however, insist that his name be Styrkar, Son of Arnkell, for the sole purpose of designating who he was to those who were the objects of his vengeance. He wanted them to know that Arnkell still sought out the enemies of the realm, even if it was through his son.

There were still his skeptics among those in the academy and in the limestone and marble palace. How could this beggar child be expected to defend against Aethelwulf and his minions, they'd laugh. Because of the urgency of the students to get on the field, matters in the realm became such that Styrkar was summoned by Kaisa to handle a suspicious affair.

Somebody had introduced plague in the water supply in an effort to weaken the city's militia and people. Kaisa told Styrkar in the utmost privacy that he was being put on the case despite the fact he was still considered in training. The decision to use him was strictly hers, she explained, and if the paladins in charge of the academy or the Lord Mayor knew of this, she would most likely face the consequences, as well as he would most likely be thrown out of the city. She had close friends in the districts, however, that would be willing to help out Styrkar so long as their names were not dragged into any mess that ensued. She also told him of her suspicions-that it was one of the cults of the Old Ones behind it and that they had help from someone close to the king. Styrkar was to find out who was responsible and get evidence and, if possible, kill those responsible.

He wasted no time. Styrkar headed directly to one of the plague stricken districts of the great golden city and into the tavern there. As he walked fearlessly into streets of the dead, he passed the burning funeral pyres of plague victims and the stink of burning human flesh wafted into his nostrils. He had smelled it before and the memories around it flooded back into his head-the riders, his mother and father's murder, the guilt. He put his hand in a pocket and caressed the metal flask hidden within that held his parents' ashes, as he turned to head back.

Then he remembered the oath to his mother and the promise to Kaisa. He had no choice in the matter-he had to do this. He turned around again and strode into the tavern. Styrkar stood out like a sore thumb and had Kaisa known that he would, she might not have asked him to do this mission. He was young and, despite skulking around the streets for two years, he was neither a bedraggled adventurer nor a stressed survivor of a plague victim. He also was taller than anyone else in the tavern.

They laughed and joked about him and a city guard pointed out his nickname of "Kaisa's Folly". It did not deter him. He calmly ordered mead and sat down at a table in a corner to study the other patrons. The teasing died off eventually when he did not respond, for he had his mind on his mission-to see if he could see anything suspicious to give him direction.

It did not take him long.

Three men walked in, all wearing black, and asked the bartender to tell "Norum" that they were here. Styrkar watched them intently and this did not go unnoticed by the city guard at the table, who blurted out a comment that "Kaisa's boy" might be homosexual. As soon as the name "Kaisa" was invoked, the men shot a surprised glance at the

Nordman before darting out the door. Without hesitation, Styrkar jolted to his feet and was out the door after them, ignoring the laughter of the other patrons. The men, once outside, drew weapons-two with daggers and one with kamas, and engaged him. Of the dagger wielders, he quickly dispatched both, but the man with the kamas proved challenging. Still, after being sliced a few times, Styrkar prevailed, sending his adversary's blood spraying onto the dirty cobblestones. He searched the bodies and found upon one of the men a note that read thusly:

> "We need to inform Norum that that bitch in the Blue Tygers is onto us. She has sent out an agent. Find out who he is and kill him if possible. I will discuss more with you when I return from Tuska."

Styrkar folded the note and slid it into a pocket on his Norlander tunic. As he looked up from his task, his eyes met with the dark ones of a man wearing a white silken masque and who sent chills into the young warrior's spine. With a flourish of his white cloak, he turned and strode off down the street. Styrkar started to run after him, but an injury to his chest from a kama began to pound furiously, forcing him to stop. The white clad man vanished around a corner in a neighborhood that could only be described as vile and unwholesome.

Styrkar realized that must be Norum.

He took the note back to Kaisa and described what had happened at the tavern. She cursed, vowing to have the head of the guards that were in the tavern that blew Styrkar's cover. But now, she had two bits of information she had not had before-that one of the villains was named Norum and that the city of Tuska to the south is somehow involved in the plague. After patching up Styrkar, she sent him off to see what he could find out about either Norum or Tuska while she relayed the information to Baldwin, the captain of her order.

This time, she saw to it her companion had protection-she had scrounged up some armor made of wolf hides for him. He returned to the district where he had seen Norum and began lurking and skulking through the alleys and shadows as he had when he begged for money and food. He saw more men dressed in black, moving furtively in the dark places he was, and he followed them in hopes they would lead him to Norum or to some place that they were working from.

After an hour and a half, they unwittingly led him to a shuttered and boarded up house with a collapsing roof and that stunk of moldy, rotting wood. Styrkar was not stupid, however, and went off to fetch Kaisa to help him broach the place. They returned within two hours time and again observed several dark men enter the building. Kaisa decided to raid the building, so the two splintered the soft, flimsy wood door and found the place filthy, rubble filled and empty of men. At first, there were no sign of footprints on the floor, but Styrkar spotted some muddy ones heading into another room. Kaisa pointed out that someone had been sloppy.

They followed the mud tracks to a wall, but they vanished there. Searching did not turn up anything immediately, but the two were undeterred as they hacked apart the wall until tore open a section that revealed a staircase. The noise had no doubt alerted the sinister inhabitants of the hidden complex below and a force of vile, long-legged dog men greeted them as they set foot into the corridor. With these, Styrkar had trouble, for the fought using alien blades with the curving before a long handle and that radiated a deviant red glow. The paladin and the nordman dispatched them, but not before the alarm had sounded and anyone important had a chance to flee out of any possible escape tunnels. Styrkar grabbed up one of the evil weapons and ran into the corridor after Kaisa. They met more of the dog men and their foul weapons, but were able to get past them after some difficulty, in one case the lady paladin receiving a head wound after her helmet had been knocked off in a skirmish.

Surely enough, the ones they sought, including Norum, had fled, but they left behind their journals and some letters as to their nefarious plans. These they confiscated and frittered away back to the academy where Kaisa and the other paladins poured over them and learned with dread the extent to which the whole scheme reached both in range of land and in the levels of power within. The perpetrators were members of a cult long since thought dead and it hinted of Aethelwulf's hand in it at some level.

Apparently, Aethelwulf had, in an effort to take over the realm of Stromgald, done something frighteningly similar, relying on the cult to undermine his predecessor and then striking out when the time was right to become the king. He then had hunted down and killed those of power who had been loyal to King Hothgar to resist any opposition. Aardsberg and others were hinted to be of interest to him now, as well as Tuska and the other border cities, and the cult moved its activities into those cities. The plans were to carry out deeds designed to demoralize the people and cause chaos, weakening the cities from within. The infection of plague in the water supply was part of this plan. It appeared Norum was the head of the cult in Aardsberg, but there was precious little mentioned about Norum except his name and something in one of the journals that insinuated he was not from these lands, although it did not give any reason for how this was known, just that he was from "an unwholesomely dreadful place".

The lady paladin and her companion were given a new objective-to hunt down Norum and find out what they could about the cult's other plans. Again, the two searched the city, starting in the district where the cult headquarters had been discovered, skulking in the shadows and alleyways. But Norum was nowhere to be found now. For that matter, the men in black ceased to be spotted as well. They prowled about for the better part of two days with no further information on Norum or the cult of the unspeakable god.

With nothing to report, Kaisa saddled up her mount and bought the young nordman a horse, the stout sort from the northern fjords with the shaggy faces that he would have been used to. Styrkar packed up his sword, battle axe, the great sword of his father and the demon blade and the two rode off for Tuska for information on Norum, the cult or any other information they could ascertain.

As they passed by a group of refugees heading for Aardsberg, Styrkar cried out upon recognizing a man from a neighboring tribe at the edge of the crowd. He was a friend of the Great Arnkell who had managed to escape the slaughter of his tribe, much as Styrkar had. His name was Thorbjorn and he was an older fellow with grey streaks in his red beard and hair. And he was tall and looked as if he had been swinging heavy weapons since he was born. Styrkar easily convinced Kaisa to let him join them on their quest. They could only find for him a jackass, but it was better than nothing at the time.

The three were off in search of the cult.

As they headed for the Spectre Wood, they passed a funeral procession heading down the road to a cemetery created for the victims of the plague. Only three dark shrouded figures followed the crude hearse made of a cargo wagon and guided by a pale horse. The driver on the wagon was a gaunt figure who was obviously in the early phases of plague-a deep hacking cough and small, purplish sores visible on his hands and face. There was no coffin. The deceased was wrapped neatly in a white blanket, although a noxious smell was carried in the wind and pale stains of yellowish green could be seen soaking through in spots.

The destination was down the road. In the cemetery, a pyre had been set up and a pit that served as a final resting place for all of the ashes awaited open wide to the sky. The undertaker waited with a torch and next to him, a priest of Trileen looked over the eulogy he had to read under the heavy, grey ceiling of clouds.

The sky had the oppressive nature and the damp smell of rain as the three descended from the plateau that the great city rested on as it overlooked the black Sea of Mystics. The road was an easy ride and they had reached the rolling hills below just as a gentle rain began to fall.

The ride across the hills took three days and Kaisa learned something interesting about the Northern Horsemen during that time. At first, it seemed as if Styrkar and Thorbjorn never slept. During the second day, she snapped out of a riding trance to notice the two horsemen were being very quiet. She glanced and noticed that they were sleeping as they rode. It was a testament to her of their horsemanship that, despite being on strange animals, the two Nordmen kept their mounts under control, even in slumber.

At the end of the third day, they had reached the edge of the Spectre Wood, a forest that had grown over an ancient and long forgotten battlefield. The three prayed to their gods before setting up camp that night, for this was no wholesome forest and there were known to be unspeakable horrors inhabiting this most unholy place.

Entering the Spectre Wood was easy enough. Since no man ventured there to cut wood, it had been spreading slowly from the original battlefield and into the hills. How the forest had become such an evil place was a mystery, although rumors abounded about strange summonings that got out of the casters' hands, various acts of cowardice and treachery and whispers of diabolic and sadistic atrocities.

There were no actual roads, but just inside the forest they found minimal underbrush, making riding through very easy. A half a mile into the forest, too, the trees were normal in all ways and were not too wide. The borders of the battlefield were very obvious, even in the darkness of the canopy-no sound of birds or tracks of animals and the trees were massive and grotesquely twisted and swollen. No light beamed through the branches despite the morning and early afternoon sun shining brightly.

What looked like fallen tree limbs were one with the leaf and moss covered ground. Kaisa dread exactly what they might be under there. The two Nordmen, especially Styrkar, had no fear in face or heart as they traversed the haunted wood. The only fear in Styrkar's heart was dying before exacting revenge upon his parents' killers and their masters.

Aside from the foreboding landscape, nothing odd occurred or was seen for the better part of the day. As they rode deeper, they began feeling the fiery penetration of eyes on their backs, yet they could hear or see nothing, not that much could be seen in that great, hideous woods.

In the late afternoon, as a pale fog started to roll in from unseen bogs and springs and streams, they came upon an ancient cemetery near ruins. Almost all of the marble stones of the building were gone, cannibalized for other buildings by unknown people ages ago or scattered about, but an idol, defaced since by time and weather, spoke that this was once a temple or a shrine, but to whom none of the visitors could figure. Most of the names on the markers had been worn away or obscured by filth and mold. Funerary urns and statues had what was left of them softened. A dreadful aura emanated from this place from somewhere within the graveyard and the horses and ass shied as they neared it. The three would make no stop here, lest the evil within was real and not perceived.

The fog grew thicker, showing diffused lights along the forest floor. They grew larger as Kaisa and the Nordmen pressed on, rising from the ground floating up out of the mist. Other spirit balls whizzed and danced about and, from the corners of their eyes, the three could see shadowy figures darting from tree to tree. The animals were panicking from the macabre spectacle to the point Styrkar and Thorbjorn had to exert great effort to control them.

They did not stop to sleep that night, riding quickly past ghosts of long dead warriors and warlocks of peculiar, unknown races resembling little or nothing of current races as they acted out the battles in which they died. Voices called out for Thorbjorn, Kaisa and Styrkar, but the three did not answer them, knowing that they did not wish to see who was the summoner.

As morning broke outside the dreadful forest, they three came upon a witch and her wagon camped among the evil trees. She looked human, but of what stock or age was unknown, and she dressed in garish colors and smelled strongly of exotic incense. She said her name was Desdinova and she greeted each of the riders by their name despite no introductions. In her hands was a decrepit deck of cards.

From the deck, she pulled the top card as she cast a cold, amber eye on Kaisa and held that card up for her to see. It depicted a bloody dagger. She told the lady paladin it was the card of the traitor and that soon, an event would happen that would cast doubt on everything she had known and force her to decide on which path she must follow.

From the deck, she pulled the top card as she cast a cold, amber eye on Thorbjorn and held that card up for him to see. It depicted a shining, gold crown. She told the elder Nordman it was the card of the king and that would come to lead the united Northern Horsemen against Aethelwulf and would become their king.

She did not pull a card from the deck as she cast a cold, amber eye on Styrkar. Desdinova told him the gods had bigger plans for him and that his role in events would be more important than could be imagined. She also warned him against powers that would seek to enslave him and use him to their ends.

Once finished, both the witch and the wagon vanished into the moist, foggy air, leaving no trace of their encounter, not even prints. The three cast apprehensive glances at each other before riding on through the haunted forest.

They found themselves fortunate that to reach Tuska they needed only to cross a small section of forest, for Tuska laid the west on the shores of the Sea of Mystics and not on the far side of the Spectre Wood, which would have taken several days to cross and requiring them to pass through the black heart of the foul woodland. They could see the delicate, white towers on the horizon as they rode into the sun and a wonderful rush of salty sea air filled their nostrils. Relief loosened their nerves and they rode more easily towards the port city.

Upon their arrival, they were too exhausted to do much in the way of hunting cults or strange men, so they bought a room at the first decent inn they came upon and collapsed upon the beds. Their dreams, however, were not pleasant ones.

In Kaisa's dream, she saw herself upon a great battlefield, but she was not leading Aardsberg's troops to glory. Rather, she was leading creatures unspeakably hideous into battle against Baldwin and the Blue Tygers. They were burning the city and a dog man spoke to her about rounding up children and from her own mouth, she heard herself order their slaughter in a sacrifice to feed something she dreaded the very name of. It was vivid, as if real, and Kaisa woke up shivering in overwhelming fear.

In Thorbjorn's dream, he saw himself leading Horsemen into a city that he could not recognize immediately and everybody within was dead. Blood pooled in the marble streets and bloated bodies choked and stank in the bronze fountains as buildings still burned. A female black knight awaited him and the Horsemen in the plaza and laughed, proclaiming them too late to save Aardsberg. Something unseen then attacked the Horsemen, spraying the walls and streets with blood and offal. It was vivid, as if real, and Thorbjorn woke up shivering in overwhelming fear.

Styrkar's sleep was merciful. His dream was of him charging into the battlefield, leading the Horsemen of Stromgald against Aethelwulf's army. He cut through line after line of demonic beasts, wading his way through blood to the grizzled, burly murderer of his family and engaged in bloody eyed fury the malevolent king. He cleaved finally into his adversary's skull, splitting his head in half and spilling out his brain, but not before Aethelwulf got in a fatal shot of his own, driving his sword into Styrkar's chest. As

Styrkar fell upon the ground, a great white light overcame him and he woke up. The dream had been so vivid as to be real and Styrkar smiled a rare broad smile.

With the disturbing-and in Styrkar's case, pleasant-dreams in mind, the three headed to the castle to speak with Tuska's Lord Mayor about the troubles of the cult. Roaming the streets, they heard word of a strange galley due in from an unknown location. Kaisa, curious, asked about this galley and a man in fancy, brocaded velvet clothes told her that the galleys would come on appointed days, bringing with them flawless gems and fine jewelry and luxurious furs of beasts that are not native to these lands. In return, they buy slaves to take back with them.

There was an oddity about the ship, for although it was a galley that looked like any other galley, it had no oars. Despite the lack of oars, the galleys moved swiftly, even when there was no wind. Furthermore, there were no marks of where it had come from and no flags for identifying its home port. And they were white. Every inch of the vessel was an eerie, deathlike white, and it was not a color that was painted on.

The men that disembarked from these vessels were repulsive as well. No one had seen their faces other than those evil, dark, burning eyes. The rest of them were robed and shrouded in that supernatural white of the ships. They made no sound when they walked and they spoke only in whispers. And they never bought food or drink at the taverns and never rested in the inns, which the owners were grateful for.

Another person, a simple dockworker, told Kaisa pretty much the same things when she inquired but added on another detail-in the hours of the night when the merchants were closed and the only business being conducted was in Tuska's brothels, the men of those strange galleys would unload strange containers and carry them to a place within the city.

After a few more inquiries that revealed not much else new, Kaisa and her friends went

to the Lord Mayor's palace, a large green marble building veined in gold and with a

massive gold dome that, on a sunny day, could be seen even from the lofty perch of

Aardsberg in the northern mountains. They were escorted to his chambers to discuss the

matters of the cult, but found him in conversation with a contingent from Murtha. The

three waited for several minutes as the arguing went back and forth and it became clear

the five scrawny men of Murtha were complaining about the treatment a suspected cult

member had been receiving in the Lord's dungeons.

Lord Kjell finally waved them off and ended the conversation, although the Murtha men

sought to continue with their near shrill protests. Several palace guards, however, herded

them out of the room. Kjell turned his attention to Kaisa and the Nordmen. The lady

paladin explained her purpose in the city-to investigate the cult's doings and to find

Norum.

It was then Kjell confided to them the events that had taken place. The man in the torture

chamber, who the Murtha men were defending and trying to gain the freedom of, had

been caught several days ago attempting to pour a bottle of blood, which Kjell suspected

was contaminated with that vile plague that was ravaging the golden city of Aardsberg,

into the city's main well. The city guards had spotted him and stopped him, but not

before he killed one with a poisoned dagger. He had been stripped and enduring torture

continuously for several days, but had revealed nothing other than he served the Dead

God.

Kjell also spoke of his concerns with the strange white galleys that came to Tuska. He

told them the description of the ships and the men and that they brought jewels and furs, but bought only slaves and never ate nor drank in the city. Kaisa told the grey-eyed king

what the simple dockworker had told her and Kjell stroked his neatly trimmed white

mustache with concern.

They spoke of Norum and Kjell believed that he may have come to Tuska, although he

was unaware of his presence, in an attempt to escape on the ghostly galley when it

arrived for its appointed trade. Another possibility was that perhaps he fled to

Aethelwulf's castle or to Murtha, in both cases becoming untouchable by any other

nation. Kjell took the three to his private chambers where he wrote a letter giving each

the authority to investigate for individuals suspected of crimes in Aardsberg.

And then he addressed the three for a favor. He sought to find out more about the galleys

and for them to find out what they could, for he believed that the ships were a pacifier,

seeking to lull the Tuskans into a false sense of security before teaming up with the cult

and attacking once the defenses were weak and unprepared. He also felt that Aethelwulf

had bit off more than he could chew with the cult if they have alliances with these

enigmatic white cloaked men. Kaisa agreed to do as he asked and requested interrogating

the prisoner to see if she could get information concerning the contamination of

Aardsberg water supplies.

Kjell had a guard guide the three into the dungeon and to the pathetic figure of a sweaty

naked man dangling from the ceiling in chains with blood flowing down his wrists and

arms. Rat bites covered his face and his entire torso was raw with flesh stripped by whips.

Blisters from burns covered his feet and legs and his genitals were bloodied and mangled.

When Kaisa addressed him, he looked at her with empty, oozing eye sockets and she jumped back in shock. When she gained her composure and questioned him about the cult and Aardsberg, he just laughed and said nothing.

Styrkar had a different approach; one that he knew Kaisa would not approve of but one he felt would work. He introduced himself as the Son of Arnkell and that he knew this man worked for Aethelwulf, the man who ordered Arnkell's death. The man's laughing ceased. Styrkar then informed him, knowing he could not see the truth, that in his possession was the bottle of contaminated blood he sought to dump in the well. Surprisingly, Kaisa did not try to step in on his questioning, so Styrkar made his threat of if he did not cooperate, he would pour the blood into every open wound and into his mouth and eyes.

The man began to talk and he told them an interesting tale of the cult and their ambitions and of Norum. Aethelwulf had indeed approached the cult to help him not only gain power, but to find an artifact to aid him. There was no clue as to where the artifact was, as it had disappeared over a thousand years ago, but he claimed the item existed and it was believed he had a supernatural entity helping him seek this item and advising him on other matters. Aethelwulf had sought out the cult to help him undermine and weaken the neighboring cities and nations for easy conquest and to allow him to extend his search beyond Stromgald.

The plague was a part of that plan. Its origins were unknown but there was a cure for it. It was clear from the cult member he had no idea where such an antidote would be kept. The disease did have a name, though-the Creeping Rot-and it would eat people from the inside out.

The last item he spoke about involved the white galleys. Only the highest echelons of the cult knew where they came from and who they were, but spoke none of that outside of their inner circle. They brought things to the cult leadership of Tuska, but those things were not kept within the city limits for long. The leadership moved whatever was brought in to a secret location someplace else and the tortured man could only surmise it was in a cave or old mineshaft.

There was nothing more the man could say, so the three left and Kaisa relayed what the cult member had told them to Kjell. Kaisa, Kjell and Thorbjorn discussed the course of action to take while Styrkar listened and decided the best thing to do would be to wait until the white galley arrived from its unknown destination to deliver its cargo to the cult. The lord also felt it was more important to execute the tortured man after the ship arrived so as to not tip off the cult members, but the fellow was not long for the world, for he died prior to the vessel's arrival and his burial was in the paupers' cemetery.

There was a strong sense of foreboding when the ship drew into the port. It was a massive, pale thing that looked like a ship of the dead. No cries of a crew could be heard calling to deckhands and dockworkers. A horrible, overpowering silence overtook the normally bustling docks and nary a soul greeted the ship. Soon, the shrouded men in white came into town with their furs and jewelry to trade for gold and slaves.

As they came ashore, Styrkar and Kaisa waited their chance and slipped on board the evil, white ship. The top deck was empty and silent with exception to an awning in the center just under the corpse white sail. Under that were pillows, elaborate rugs and hookah pipes. Not far was a hatch and the two climbed down into the lower decks.

The first deck was also vacant except for the staterooms of the merchants, which were close in furnishings to the awning on the main deck-ornate rugs, hookah pipes, and silken pillows. They realized, too, the place was lit up by some permanent magic spell, for not a candle or lamp could be seen anywhere, yet it was as bright as day. Everything was white like the rest of the ship, but there were no signs of any crew quarters or ship records anyplace.

The lower deck was where one group of oarsmen should have been, but the deck was again bare except for one room that was full of blood and gore on the walls, with a butcher block and a large cleaver, all encrusted with dried blood. A shriveled finger laid on the floor and spoke of what sort of food was eaten aboard this ship and the others as well. The other decks, too, proved barren with no oarsmen and only the scantest of cargo holds and empty slave cages that would soon be full of slaves who would be provisions for the strange merchants in white.

It was on the bottom deck that they discovered the mystery behind the ship's movement. A strange device of delicate, brass-like metal and silver gears sat in the middle of the completely barren deck and hummed in evil contentment. On the floor, was a reddish brown stain and it became instantly clear that the slaves were not just for food.

They turned to leave and were face to face with one of the men in white, his dark eyes burning into them. Both went for their weapons, but he passed a hand through the air and both dropped into a deep sleep of haunted dreams.

When they awoke, they were laying on the floor of one of the cells and could hear murmurs and smell the stench of sweat and dirt from slaves. Styrkar and Kaisa were still armed, but found they could not move from laying on their backs. Outside their cage stood one of the merchants, looking in with hateful eyes. Kaisa went to address him, but found her voice paralyzed by the same magick that held her and Styrkar to the floor. They laid there for what felt like an eternity, unable to move or talk. They were hungry and thirsty, but no food or water was brought to them. When they slept, their dreams were overtaken by nightmares so terrible that they could not bear the thought of slumber, fighting to keep their eyes open. They could hear from the upper deck, from that horrible blood stained room, screams of slaves being butchered and the heaviness of fear weighed in their hearts.

Finally, they felt the ship rocking and scraping as it came into port. Several merchants came to the cell and yanked them unceremoniously out, forcing them to their feet as the spells were removed and new ones were cast with waves and gestures of their hands. They were taken to the top deck and a strange cage of white light formed around them. The merchants then disembarked, leaving them standing bleary eyed and silent.

The most disturbing thing to finally hit Kaisa's mind was that there were no slaves in the cages and none were on the decks below waiting to be sold. Her and Styrkar were the only cargo and apparently important enough that they were not used for food or to fuel this demonic ship.

The land beyond the docks, which bustled with strange creatures they never knew existed and were frightful to behold, was the most barren land they had ever seen. There were no mountains or no hills, no rivers or lakes. Nothing but flat, barren sand reflecting light so that it seemed to glow with the flames of hell. The heat made worse their thirst as they awaited their fate.

The sun never seemed to set here and it was with horror that Styrkar and Kaisa came to realize they were no longer on their home plane. They did not know where they were, but strongly suspected, by the great bronze minarets and domes, there was a possibility that it was someplace in the Great Abyss.

The merchants eventually returned with a large being with black fur covering its body and a face that was half dog and half baboon and with eight arms and the lower body of a giant asp. It wore layers of red and black brocade and it regarded the two with brass, iris-less eyes.

The thing laughed deeply and slowly and thanked Kaisa for bringing Styrkar to him, for not only had she brought the greatest threat to him, but because the young Nordman was not fully trained, she had brought potentially the greatest warrior. With training, Styrkar, the son of the one man who could have defeated him, would be his greatest servant, for Styrkar's mother was not exactly human and her son must have inherited her powers at least in part. Of what, however, the beast thing either did not know or refused to tell and Kaisa and Styrkar's voices were still paralyzed so that they could not ask.

It explained that it was looking for a powerful artifact and had hoped teaming up with Aethelwulf would have helped meet that end. However, Aethelwulf was more concerned about ruling the entire known world and the artifact, although important in achieving that goal, was not necessary enough for the moment for treacherous tyrant to hunt it down expeditiously. As a result, he had hired cults of obscure Dead God to carry out the search and retrieval of the artifact, but had not been aggressively following it. Instead, he also diverted some of the vital manpower needed to find the artifact into poisoning wells and causing chaos so that the search was being carried out on his end short handed. The demonic beast needed the artifact quickly, for it had the power to allow his to travel to other planes to gather and transport armies to those planes. He was tiring of Aethelwulf's fooling around about it and would be quite reasonable; he grinned an abnormally long grin, and offered the two something to work for him. He then freed the two from the spells with a wave of one of his clawed hands.

Kaisa went for her sword, but was surprised to see Styrkar rubbing his chin and his brow furrowed in thought. His desire for revenge against Aethelwulf and his minions was overbearing and he told this thing his price to do the deed-he wanted all responsible for his parents' deaths to meet him in battle to face his wrath. This request took even the beast by surprise, for Kaisa suspected he was hoping Styrkar would ask for a powerful weapon or gold, as most men would do. It would be granted, the creature promised, when Styrkar finished the quest and was ready to handle the evil king and his champions.

The creature looked at the lady paladin, for Styrkar's deal put her in a difficult position-helping the demon achieve such power was strictly against her beliefs, but her growing love of Styrkar made it difficult, too, to refuse. He told Styrkar to go ashore and eat and rest up to prepare for the quest and the young Nordman did so. Then the thing turned his attention back to Kaisa and made an offer of his own, even though she spoke nothing of her conflict, he could see it in her eyes. H e made an offer of his own- her and Styrkar's souls. If she accepted and succeeded, they would be free to go to Valhalla upon death. But if she refused or the failed, they would be forever tied to him to fulfill his whims and desires for all eternity.

Kaisa reluctantly accepted to find his artifact and was allowed to rest up and prepare for the quest.

The port city was large and full of inhabitants even more bizarre than the men in white and their master. It resembled the cities of the great southern deserts of Kaisa and Styrkar's own world and was overpowering with the perfume of incense. The streets were tiled in stone of red and gold and brass statues and fountains that were filled with hideous, colorful water creatures that Kaisa was not sure if they were fish or amphibians. The gold marble and alabaster and brimstone buildings were carved with scenes of debauchery and damned souls and the more Kaisa viewed these, the more convinced that she and Styrkar were in the Abyss.

They fed in a tavern on a bright yellow, fragrant soup and drank a sweet, red wine, while Kaisa decided it was time to talk to her friend and find out more about him, since now it seemed he was to be a key player in what was unfolding in the fate of humanity. He had drunk several glasses of the maddeningly potent wine and spoke quite freely of his past. Most of what he said of Arnkell and Astrid was well known by her already-they met on a battlefield and she was a sword maiden of Fantoft and that they had one child and that they were two of the most respected and feared warriors of the Nordlands.

But then he began to tell her things she did not know-that his mother's true origins were not clearly known. She had lived in Fantoft, to be sure, but that she had been born to parents in a place no human has seen and that is near the tallest mountain in the coldest and most treacherous of regions in the mystical frigid wastelands the border the Nordlands to the north. This was a revelation to Kaisa, for it had always been believed that the Nordlands were the northernmost populated lands and that above them was most likely frozen seas. Styrkar went on to explain that those unmentioned lands are the realms of creatures, gods, too powerful for mere men to deal with and too complex to comprehend, so the Nordlanders never speak of them beyond their lands. They called it the Lands of the Evernight and not even the bravest men crossed into them for fear of incurring the wrath of those things that dwell there, with exception of one man. That man was Arnkell Darkhorse. And only then, he did so because he had found a guide in Fantoft, Astrid, to take him there. Styrkar described the place they had gone as a mountain higher than any mountain in the known world and upon which the gods dwell in order to hide from mortals who seek them. He did not say why they had gone there. After the quest, Arnkell married Astrid, who was more beautiful than any maiden in the Nordlands with her flowing white hair and eyes so blue that they glowed. They had Styrkar and were raising him to be a warrior in accordance to the Norns, although for what purpose they had told his parents he did not say even when asked several times, when the soldiers of Aethelwulf descended upon the village and killed everybody but Styrkar, a feat that he attributed to his being knocked unconscious while attempting to repel their invasion and left for dead. He had witnessed before that, though, his father's death. Upon waking, he found his father had been beheaded and his mother was mortally wounded and it was to her he vowed to avenge them. After he accomplished his vengeance, he only would seek death in battle so he could leave this world as honorably as he could.

Kaisa then asked him why he decided to make the deal with a fiend to find the artifact. She was more curious over anything else. Styrkar told her that it was more important he would find whatever means to get to Aethelwulf.

They went to an inn and were taken to a room that was larger than all the other room except the common one on the first floor. It had walls covered in red and gold cloth brocaded with ornate, perverted patterns and luxurious soft furs covered the floors and the great round bed. There were no windows and the room was illuminated by floating orbs of red lights and the smell of incense was oppressive.

Although the two only had a small amount of the wine, they found themselves woozy-headed and that whatever reservations they had about each other were gone. They crawled naked into the bed and, in the blood red glow of the orbs, they made passionate love before drifting off into a wine-induced, haunted sleep.

In the morning, they awoke cleaned up, fully clothed and armored and with their weapons under an awning of red cloth and on ornate rugs covering the red, burning sand. Next to them were two water skins, two sacks of dried, red fruit and a note.

The note was inscribed in an elongated handwriting and it said:

> *"A map to the artifact's location you must find is in the desert. It is in the ruins of those who have dwelled long before any of my kind came to this land. Follow the cliffs and you shall find the ruins. It is, however, unfortunate, that in all of my searching, I have yet to find the cliffs, let alone the ruins. I spotted them once but when I awoke, they were no longer to be seen. When you have found this map, I shall send you to your plane to retrieve my artifact. Do not think of reneging on our deal, for I will make your souls suffer dearly."*

They looked around and could see no cliffs peering up over the dunes of the barrens wastes. One horizon looked like the other with no way to distinguish one from the other-no landmarks, no plants, and no roads. There were no footprints leading to or from the awning. They went out and crested a dune to see if anything could be spotted anywhere, but quickly became disoriented in the heat and sun glare that they could not find the awning again.

So, with no other options, they commenced with their search for the cliffs. Without a compass, they could not figure which direction they were traveling in and it seemed as if the sun was never going to set, so time was indiscernible. They walked for what seemed to be hours, running out first of water, then food and eventually finding themselves crawling across the scorching sands.

The first thought upon seeing palm trees was that they were hallucinating until Styrkar managed to put a trembling hand upon a trunk. They noticed amid several palm trees a low crude, black rock dome. There was an arched opening on one side and they crawled in to hear the trickling of water. It was an oasis and they drank and filled their water skins and rested until they were able to get onto their feet again and start out to hunt down the cliffs. Styrkar figured that the stone had to come from someplace and figured they were headed in the right direction for something.

Once again, when they wandered into the desert, they found the oasis seemed to get lost behind them. A breeze suddenly appeared and provided some relief from the heat. After a while, it was evident it was a constant breeze from the northwest. Something told Styrkar to walk into the direction of the breeze. Kaisa followed him.

Their shadows finally grew long, betraying the oncoming of night, however slow. On the horizon they first saw what appeared to be three mountains. As they approached, it became obvious they were not mountains but man made structures-pyramids. In fact, they were pyramids larger than any Kaisa had ever seen or heard of before and the breezes grew ever stronger as they approached, as if all the winds of this desert came from there. They arrived at the base of one and the winds blew strongly from it. The pyramids were three colors-one being pure white marble, one being black basalt and one being made of stones as red as the sands. Each was covered with carved runes in a language neither Kaisa not Styrkar could read and each had one, yawning entrance. The wind from the red one was torrid. The wind from the black stunk of ashes. The wind from the white was freezing. The three were equidistant from each other and, between the three, was a colossus of a large creature that they could not recognize and resembled nothing in their world. None of the four structures were damaged or defaced and the two determined these were not the ruins they sought, for no cliffs were near them. Nevertheless, there was no harm in investigating these mysterious tombs.

Then the statue spoke to them in a voice that sounded as if it were every soul in the Abyss speaking at once and it told them they must pass the Challenge of the Pyramids. If they refused, the consequences would be immediate and fatal. If they lost, their souls would take the place of the entity that defeated them, in the form of the original entity, until they defeated a challenger. Should they win a part of the challenge, they would be healed and forced on to the next part of the challenge until all three of the pyramids' challenges were completed. Should they succeed, they would receive a reward. The contest would begin when the two chose a pyramid and would end if the two stepped out of the final pyramid victorious.

Styrkar decided upon the black one first and Kaisa followed him down the stairs within. At the base of the stairs, they were attacked by two shadow mastiffs. The dogs tore into them, but were unable to defeat them. The two warriors were able to fight them off and kill the shadow beasts with much difficulty. When both dogs were dead, the door before them opened and they could hear the door at the top of the stairs grind closed.

The next room was bathed in a purple glow and red runes covered the black floor onto which their blood left drops. The entire place smelled of ash, which became more evident to be from the rocks themselves than from anything actually burning, for the light source of this room were glowing purple orbs levitating near the ceiling. A very tall man in heavy black armor stood in the center of the room within a ring of the red runes. His hands rested upon a great axe and he set his ancient eyes upon his visitors. They fully expected him to attack them, but instead he asked them to pick one of the three doors behind him. Along the wall behind him were the three doors in a row. Kaisa asked him about the doors, wondering why they had to choose, but the man did not answer. Styrkar again made the choice. He chose the one to the left.

The door on the left opened and Styrkar and Kaisa entered the corridor beyond. At the end was a chamber and in the chamber was a circle of pedestals above which floated items surrounded in indigo light. One was a battleaxe of iridescent black metal and a handle of dragon bone. One was a helmet fashioned into the shape of a dragon skull. One was a spell book, whose cover bore the darkened, flat face of a skinned man. One was a silver ring that bore no marks upon it. One was a vial of a blood red liquid. One was a mace of shining gold. One was a suit of black armor. A man in a black robe came forth into the circle and told them to choose one item for their challenge. Styrkar again made the choice. He chose the ring for its plainness.

A door opened in a far corner of the room as Styrkar grabbed the ring. He offered it to Kaisa, but she declined, hoping that whatever magic in it was powerful enough to save him from whatever lurked in that room. So, he put on the ring and there was an indigo flash and he turned into a ghostly form glowing blue.

This was not a room but a maze and the walls were of a metal polished to a mirror finish. Kaisa suddenly became aware of tickles on those parts of her legs not covered in metal armor. She looked down and found herself being covered in spiders. Her heart froze and she must have screamed, for Styrkar had raced back to her and began beating the arachnids off of her. She would have helped if she had not froze entirely, gazing into a memory of her as a child crying with swollen hands and face and several spiders crawling upon her skin. It was Styrkar's yelling that snapped her out of it and she finally began swatting the creatures off herself. It took a few minutes, but the spiders were gone not only from her, but from the maze as well.

They continued through the maze when they heard other footsteps ahead. The two paused to listen and ready their weapons. From around the corner stepped the tall figure of Aethelwulf. Styrkar's heart froze, but he acted instinctively, for he had seen this in his mind and dreams for over two years and had planned how he would eventually handle his foe. He sprung forth with a battle cry and the two commenced into heavy, hate-filled melee. When Kaisa tried to run to his aid, an invisible barrier stopped her and she was only able to watch helplessly as the tyrant cleaved into him mercilessly, although he was giving every inch he was getting in brutality. There was a scream and Aethelwulf tensed up, dropping his sword, which oddly did not clang as it fell. The bloodied king faded from sight and Styrkar and Kaisa were suddenly outside in the hot desert twilight, fully healed and standing before the massive statue again.

Then the statue spoke again to them in a voice that sounded as if it were every soul in the Abyss speaking at once and it told them they must pass the Challenge of the Pyramids. If they refused, the consequences would be immediate and fatal. If they lost, their souls would take the place of the entity that defeated them, in the form of the original entity, until they defeated a challenger. Should they win a part of the challenge, they would be healed and forced on to the next part of the challenge until all three of the pyramids' challenges were completed. Should they succeed, they would receive a reward. The contest continued and they had to choose the next pyramid and the contest would end if the two stepped out of the final pyramid victorious.

This time, Kaisa chose the pyramid and decided upon the white one with its frigid winds and Styrkar followed her down the stairs, putting on the ring that turned him into a spectre. At the base of the stairs, they were attacked by two winter wolves. This time, they fought the beasts off quickly, but not before suffering damage to their freezing breaths. When both dogs were dead, the door before them opened and they could hear the door at the top of the stairs grind closed.

The next room was bathed in a bluish glow and black runes covered the white floor as they entered, trembling and frost bitten. A mist filled the place from the cold and in the center of the chamber stood a scantily clad, blue-skinned maiden with long, flowing white hair. She greeted the two pleasantly by name and told them she had a gift for each of them to use in their challenge that, if they passed, they could keep.

In her left hand, she gave Styrkar a battleaxe that glowed blue and felt cold to the touch. In her right, she gave Kaisa a long sword that faintly showed white and felt cold to the touch. Once both held the weapons in their hands, two doors in the wall behind the woman opened up and Styrkar was to go in the left and Kaisa in the right.

Again they stepped into mazes, only now they were each in a different one. The walls of this maze were of ice too thick and ancient to see through. The place was freezing cold, but Styrkar felt at home in it despite still being frozen from the winter wolves.

He heard footsteps and at first thought he was hearing Kaisa nearby, but before long realized that the sounds were coming towards him. Through the icy mists stepped his father Arnkell and Styrkar looked confused at him. Then the great Nordman swung his great sword, which weirded Styrkar out as he knew he carried that very weapon upon his back. He dodged and the blade whistled past his head and it dawned upon him that this must be a demon that looked like his father. He put aside any reservations about attacking his father and flung himself into battle with this mimic. It was a long, drawn out battle as the two sprayed the ice with each other's blood, but again, Styrkar was victorious and he dragged his bloody body along in the maze, the axe he had been given covered in gore, but still glowing coolly.

Kaisa heard footsteps ahead of her and paused to see who was coming. After a minute, Styrkar strode out of the icy mist towards her. At first, she smiled at him in relief, but it quickly faded as she noticed he did not have that fiery life in his blue eyes. They were dead, cold and staring as he drew his battle axe and charged her. Putting aside her inhibition of fighting her lover, she hefted her sword into him as he hacked into her with all of his strength. The battle lasted some time before she succeeded in killing him, tears flowing down her face as she prayed it was not him. An overwhelming white light overtook her and she found herself standing next to him outside of the pyramids and before the statue, both fully healed again. She threw her arms around him and embraced him for several minutes.

Then the statue spoke again to them in a voice that sounded as if it were every soul in the Abyss speaking at once and it told them they must pass the Challenge of the Pyramids. If they refused, the consequences would be immediate and fatal. If they lost, their souls would take the place of the entity that defeated them, in the form of the original entity, until they defeated a challenger. Should they win a part of the challenge, they would be healed and forced on to the next part of the challenge until all three of the pyramids' challenges were completed. Should they succeed, they would receive a reward. The contest continued and they had to enter the red pyramid and the contest would end if the two stepped out of it victorious.

So the two entered the red pyramid and descended the stairs within. At the base of the stairs, they were attacked by two hell hounds. The hounds spit fire that caused the skins of the two humans to blister and throb in excruciating pain. Still, they fought the dogs and, after a few minutes, killed them. When both dogs were dead, the door before them opened and they could hear the door at the top of the stairs grind closed.

They walked into a hazy room that glowed red and smelled of burning flesh. The red floor was covered in ash, but the white runes that lay beneath could be seen here and there. In the center of the room was a great red wyrm that was more hideous and diabolic than any dragon they had heard of in legends. He said his name was H'rzz'gaar, the son of an ancient female red dragon and a demon lord. About his chamber were chests and piles of gold and red gems, but only one door behind him. H'rzz'gaar made it clear the only way to that door was through him. The dragon fiend told them, too, that should they defeat him that any or all of his hoard is theirs to do with as they pleased.

He then shot forth a stream of fire that sent Kaisa and Styrkar diving away in opposite directions to the floor. As the lady paladin landed with a grunt, H'rzz'gaar swept into her with his massive plated tail and threw her into the wall with great force. Despite having her armor on, pain rushed from within her and she landed in a heap, the wind knocked out of her. Styrkar had escaped the flame but not the claws and they rended blistered flesh from his left arm and torso and ripped the armor from him. H'rzz'gaar glanced at Kaisa with baleful eyes, as if to make certain she was still down, and continued its attack on Styrkar.

The beast struck like as asp to bite at the Nordman. Styrkar rolled aside and drove his glowing battle axe into the dragon's face with all of his might, anchoring it deep into bone and causing H'raa'gaar to howl as if all of the Abyss had broken free. He threw his head up and Styrkar held on with a white knuckled grip to the handle of his axe, even as the dragon him around to shake him off.

Kaisa watched on as she managed to find a weapon poking its handle out of a nearby mound of coins. It was a gold axe that glowed a furious red and sent courses of pain and fire through her blistered, broken body as she grasped it. Agonizing from the weapon's power and from her internal bleeding, she crawled along to the dragon's tail and chopped its plated end off with several angry swings. As expected, H'rzz'gaar spun around to attack this new threat. As it did, Styrkar took up his sword in his blood soaked left hand and began hacking furiously on the beast's face. Again, it frantically shook its head, this time flinging the Nordman from his face.

Kaisa had had the chance to crawl under the fiendish serpent's belly as it dealt with Styrkar's violent attacks. Taking the axe, which still burned all through her, she cleaved at the underbelly, tearing open the dragon's abdomen. The dragon jumped back and

exposed Kaisa to his attack. He began clawing at her, missing mostly as she dropped the

axe and began scurrying about the floor and behind treasure heaps and chests.

Styrkar had landed painfully into a large pile of items. Sorely crawling along on it, two

things happened to him. First, he noticed laying amid the debris of a broken chest some

weapons glowing a faint cobalt blue. One was a handsome long sword covered in runes

he could not read. The other was a beautifully crafted composite bow next to which was a

single red arrow. He took both and crawled forward to attack H'rzz'gaar when he did the

second thing entirely by accident.

There was a sharp pain in his left hand and he yanked it back to examine the injury,

seeing a yellow-green liquid covering his palm and reddish glow from the chamber's

braziers reflecting like lights off of bits of glass on his skin. He could feel a rush through

him and a tingling in all of his limbs and wounds. The cuts from the glass in his hand and

the deep gashes from the dragon's claws began to close before his eyes and the blisters

flattened and vanished. Energy flowed through him as he tore off the remaining scraps of

armor and ran up on H'rzz'gaar, praying to his gods it was not too late to save Kaisa. The

demon dragon did not expect him to attack from behind. And not with that sword and that

arrow.

Styrkar swung the sword into an arc into what part of the dragon's body he could reach,

the blade biting viciously into the scales. Again, the great beast howled as if the Abyss

had broken free and spun around to attack, Styrkar dropped the sword and backed up

quickly, nocking the arrow as he did. As H'rzz'gaar lunged at him, he fired off the red

arrow from the bow he had appropriated. It was a special arrow and one H'rzz'gaar had forgotten about entirely over the ages and once free in the air, that arrow sought out his left eye and went into that eye with a sickening squish.

H'rzz'gaar bellowed even more loudly and painfully than before, raising up on his hind legs and trying to yank the fatal arrow out of his eye socket. But a transformation had begun. First his head started to turn to sand, followed by the rest of his body and the winds of the pyramids blew it out the door that opened up as H'rzz'gaar died. Beyond the threshold were stairs leading up.

Styrkar ran to Kaisa, who was on the floor and bleeding profusely from gashes inflicted upon her by the fiendish dragon and from her mouth from internal injuries. He began searching the large chests and treasure piles until he found another vial of the liquid he saw dripping from his hand. He took in his left hand that vial to Kaisa as she gasped, her breaths rattling and gurgling in her throat, and took in his right hand her head as he poured the liquid into her mouth and over her wounds. She could feel a rush through her and a tingling in all of her limbs and within her body. She watched as the gashes and burns on her arms and hands closed and vanished and she was soon able to stand.

Collecting his battle axe, which had fallen to the floor when H'rzz'gaar turned to dust, and his other weapons, Styrkar searched for more of the vials, for new armor and for arrows for his bow. The Nordman found several vials and ignored any that did not match the liquid of the one he crushed. He also found studded leather armor of a reddish brown color that smelled like both sulphur and a dog and two quivers of arrows, one with long knives with ornate black handles sheathed in slots upon the outside. Kaisa, remembering too sorely the axe she had grabbed, feared to touch the stuff for fear it was all weapons of the Abyss.

Once Styrkar was ready, the two ascended up and into the cold desert night.

The statue then the statue spoke again to them in a voice that sounded as if it were every soul in the Abyss speaking at once and it told them they passed the Challenge of the Pyramids. As they had won the challenge, they would receive a reward. A creature that looked like a black dog with red on its muzzle and hands and wearing a black and red robe of sinister swirls appeared before them with a most ornately carved box of black wood and held it out to Kaisa.

She took the box and opened it. Within was a round, brass device with a face that showed the four directions. The voice told them that the device was a compass, which Kaisa knew, but it pointed to no pole. It pointed to the thing that they sought-the ruins where the map that Baat'zaar, the demonic sultan who sent them on this quest, had sought was hidden.

The statue then spoke no more and Kaisa and Styrkar followed the compass into the cold, starless night. Strange creatures lurked the lands once the hot sun was down and the sands cooled. There were many of them, most too hideous to describe, but none if any showed an interest in two heavily armed humans running across the desert in search of ruins.

The sun was coming up, painting the sky in unholy waves of crimson and azure, when the two spotted the great cliffs on the horizon.

The first sign of the ruins they came upon was the remains of a colossus that appeared human in design, but whose features were mostly worn off from sand and time. All that remained of it was a half buried head and two half buried feet and no inscription left of who it was or what it commemorated. The face looked familiar, but neither Kaisa nor Styrkar could place it.

Beyond the fallen colossus, around a mile away, they came upon the ruins of a city. Once gleaming, colorful towers and domes were mostly collapsed and skeletal. Temples lied defaced and razed, telling of the great city's brutal death. Shells of houses and large debris poked up from the sand like bones of the dead and everything had been bleached and eroded by the sun and torrid winds. Neither beasts nor birds came to this place and there was silence and that eerie, peaceful aura of a graveyard-a feeling Styrkar knew all too well from his own village when he cremated his mother and father.

The compass guided them past ruin after ruin until it indicated one great tower in particular. Most of the colorful dome had collapsed and faded, but the door to the place yawned to them. Inside, there was an empty chamber with stairs going both up and down. The furniture, although broken, was still here in the light coming in through the door and the shadows of the two warriors fell long on them. The wood and cloth were dry and brittle, but still displayed a defined hint of the lavish tastes the beings that dwelled here had.

They climbed the stairs, but rubble from the destroyed upper floors filled the floor above and blocked their way. As they came back down, it became apparent that it was not just sand all over the floors and furniture, but dust from the bulging ceiling.

They descended the stairs and into a dark basement. Styrkar used his sword's blue light to guide him and Kaisa through the room. There was more destroyed furniture and sand around the floor and evidence that at some point, creatures, possibly intelligent, had used this place for shelter, although they had long since left this place. Still, though, they had left trash and bones and a bed roll, now infested with sand fleas that were visible even in the blue glow.

Then to the surprise of the lady paladin and the Nordman was the discovery of a trap door with a ring latch. They opened it and found a crude ladder leading into a sub-basement. Without hesitation, they descended the ladder into the darkness.

The room below was very well preserved with a mosaic of a summoning circle and runes in lapis and coral and obsidian tiles on the floor and bookshelves full of tomes and scrolls, although the writing was foreign and unreadable. A book sat on a podium and, from what Kaisa could make from turning its delicate vellum pages that it was a book on magic, possibly summoning. Two elaborately carved chests sat against the wall and were unlocked, as if the person who had this place practiced clandestinely but knew it would never be discovered.

Styrkar opened the chests and found in one robes and books, although none of the books proved to be anything useful to him. He guessed they were spell books of sorts by the runes inscribed upon them. The second chest held scrolls, but again, they appeared to be spells, not maps. Kaisa looked at the compass and found it spinning oddly. The two climbed up and got pieces of broken furniture to use as torches and they commenced searching the room for hidden compartments or doors.

Then something on the ceiling caught Styrkar's attention, being he stood closer to the ceiling than Kaisa. He held his torch up and saw it. The map. Painted on the ceiling in vivid colors that were chipping off in areas, but the important areas were there. Kaisa grabbed a scroll and burned a piece of what looked like a stick of wood for a spell component in her torch to create a writing stick. She copied the design while Styrkar held his torch up and moved it as needed. Once finished, they extinguished the torches and left the ruins.

Kaisa and Styrkar followed the cliffs to see where they would take them. At one point, they heard strong winds and guessed the pyramids were not far off, although they could not see them. Again, night fell in the desert and this time, the two found a niche in the base of the cliffs to sleep, ignoring the sounds of the beasts that lurked the sands in the dark.

In the morning, they decided to chance going into the desert again, leaving the cliffs and knowing full well that they would lose sight of them and see that sameness of the horizon in all directions again. They had walked for hours when a lone figure appeared on the horizon walking towards them. They stopped and watched through sweat-burning, squinted eyes, but neither went for their weapons. As it drew near, they could see the creature was one of Baat'zaar's minions in white. When it was about close enough, it waved its hand and a bolt of light hit the blood red sands, leaving behind a red vortex. The white shrouded creature gestured for them to enter it.

They did so and found themselves in an alley in Tuska. It was night and very cool compared to the otherworldly desert they had just left. Dazed and tired, they sought out an inn and spent the night there before reporting to Kjell and Thorbjorn the next day. Kaisa took the time to request an ink well and parchment and to make a more permanent copy of the map.

The next day, the two went to Kjell and found Thorbjorn there and they told them about Baat'zaar and his ships and his request that they find an artifact for him. They told of the pyramids and the ruins and were surprised to hear Kjell recognized the descriptions. He explained that others have spoken of those places and that such stories were said to have been originated from those men in white that rode the morbid white ships. When they showed him the map, he reacted in a way that made Styrkar, Thorbjorn and Kaisa very uneasy. The Lord told them the place was the Unholy City in the south in the middle of the Endless Wastes. Evil things had been said to dwell there, more powerful than any man had ever known. If they wanted to go, he'd offer a ship to take them south, but that he could not with a clear conscience, send any of his people there to accompany them. Thorbjorn, however, had no fear of following the two into the Wastes to retrieve the artifact.

So, one of Kjell's ships took them down the coast to the lands of the newer kingdoms. The journey took several days and was uneventful. During that time, Kaisa worked on her relationship with Styrkar in addition to talking with both Nordmen about their journey to the Endless Wastes and the Unholy City.

They arrived in the port city of Takros and bought horses with money Kjell gave them for the journey. They spent two days getting what they needed and rode into the heartland of the new kingdom Arkanis. The lands were lush and green and the weather was much warmer than their homes up north, although not as hot as the desert they had been in or the one they were headed to. Near the city were farmlands and some folks stared as the three strangers rode past. None came to talk to them or wave to them. It made Kaisa and Thorbjorn nervous, but Styrkar seemed oblivious to it.

The entire ride from Takros to the mountains took a day and by the middle of the night, they had crossed the rolling hills and arrived before the mountain range, where they camped for the night. Unlike previous journeys, the Nordmen had not slept during their ride and the three took turns watching the campsite.

When Styrkar sat up on his duty, he was studying the map Kaisa drew when something caught his eye. There was a movement in the darkness and his first instinct was to kick Thorbjorn's hand, waking the burly warrior from a dream. They watched for it from the camp, not willing to leave Kaisa alone, especially in these strange lands and after the farm folks had been glaring at them so. They both saw it the second time and both swore it looked like a person, but it was leaving the area quickly, so they decided against chasing it.

When the morning sun rose into the cloudless sky, the three began their arduous journey into the Grey Mountains. The first day, the three rode past a closed mine from which unholy noises could be heard emanating from. They did not stop. Further along the trail, they came upon an abandoned mining village and felt phantom eyes penetrating their backs. They did not stop.

That night, Styrkar and Thorbjorn saw the thing running in the night again, this time on the cliff across the chasm next to which they camped and recognized it as definitely a human, but who they had no idea yet.

The next day, as they rode, they spoke of it with Kaisa, explaining that they were not sure of what it was when they first saw it, but now they were certain that this person was following them. She was concerned and asked them to awaken her the next time that they saw this person.

That day, they found ruins of one of the kingdoms that preceded Arkanis and the other new kingdoms. They were not the ruins of humans, but of something bigger and more frightening to think about. They stopped to look these over, even though there were not much of them left. Kaisa sketched the ruins in her journal and inscribed notes on them. It was here that all three spotted their stalker creeping around rocks above and could make out that he wore the clothes, or seemed to wear the clothes, of those from the desert folks- long, dark robes and a shemagh. A sick feeling crept through their veins at the thought that the dwellers of the sands would be involving themselves in the quest.

The three rode on and, on the fourth day, found the foliage of the mountains changing and becoming sparse. They passed nothing unusual, but still noticed the desert man lurking about. They decided against confronting him yet, however, because he was not interfering with their quest. It was also hoped that he would attract the attention of any curious or hungry wild animals or roving bandits that would otherwise be focused on the threesome.

The fifth day, they came upon a river that fed from the Grey Mountains and flowed beyond the mountain range and into the desert. They followed it, but took care not to drink from it or eat the fish that swam in it or any of the foliage that grew on its shores, for it was said that the river passed through an accursed place and was most unholy. Further along the banks they traveled, the trees grew scarce and more sinister in their twisting trunks and gnarled, claw-like branches. Through the peaks, they could spot the distant horizon of the Wastes.

The sixth day, they came upon a lichen encrusted basalt pillar left behind by an ancient civilization, although which one they did not know. The planet was very old and many preceded man as its masters and residents. Kaisa again sketched the pillar and copied the alien writings and images upon it. And again, they spotted the desert man, only now, his actions were different. He had drawn in closer than he had before and he seemed intent upon trying to make out from a distance what the lady paladin was doing.

This behavior did not bode well for Styrkar in the slightest. He decided that the desert man needed to be dealt with and excused himself from the others, not revealing his intentions to them. He walked into some nearby bushes, pretending to play with his belt, but once out of earshot and eye sight, he crept silently along the rocks and brush until he came out behind and above the lurker. The fellow was of swarthy skin and sported a long beard of black ringlets. As he observed the man, he noticed he was taking notes in elongated handwriting on a scroll using a bit of charcoal.

Styrkar's stomach knotted up and his skin crawled. He was not so dumb to know a bad thing when he saw it. He had heard of the desert folks and their rigid intolerance and surmised that whoever this nosy person was, his attention was not in the best interest of the three. From the quiver with the two black-handled daggers, Styrkar took an arrow and he fired it from that bow he had found in the Challenge of the Red Pyramid, striking the spy in his neck. The desert man gasped with a gurgle and fell forward, tumbling down to the river bank with Styrkar, whistling, a rare act for the dour Nordman, and gingerly leaping down the steep slope behind him to his startled companions.

He explained to them why he had killed this lurker who had been tailing them since they journeyed into the mountains as he searched the broken body. In his dark robes, he found more scrolls, which he burned later that night in their camp fire, and, on one of the man's fingers, a gold ring with that curved, elongated script that the lurker had used in his scrolls. Styrkar took the ring and dropped it into his belt pouch with a soft clang as it struck the metal flask of his parents' ashes. Kaisa raised an eyebrow to this sound, but said nothing. Once finished with the dead man, Thorbjorn threw the body into the river so the cursed waters carried it away.

The body had drifted away some distance down the river and was well out of eye sight when the three resumed traveling. They did not see the black tentacle rise up from the murky waters, wrap itself around the corpse's torso and yank it under the water with a soft sploosh. Whatever the horror was that lurked there did not surface when the three riders passed, preferring to feed on the desert man's cadaver.

Late the next day, as streams of crimson and violet streaked the sky in dramatic, violent waves, they entered the Fingers of Blood, the land of tors of stark red stone. They camped near the river that night and reviewed the map Kaisa drew from the ruins. It was decided that, against their better judgment, they would stop at Al-Zar, the merchant city, for any supplies they needed to venture into the desert.

The next day, they rode for Al-Zar, but at noon, the heat became unbearable. The three set up a tent and waited until the late afternoon brought cooler temperatures. After that, the three traveled by night until they reached Al-Zar deep in the land of the pale sands.

Al-Zar's existence was hardly a mystery compared to the ruins Styrkar and Kaisa had been in or the place that the three now traveled to. It rose from an oasis and was a stopover for merchant caravans traveling between the southern and south eastern cities of the deserts and far mountains and the north western cities of ice and snow and fjords. Many buildings in Al-Zar were painted garishly or were tiled with colorful, glazed mosaics. Some had new layers of gypsum slurry smeared and brushed upon them. Merchant booths and tables lined streets full of veiled men and women and the air wafted with the burning sweetness of incense mingling with the aromas of pungent spices and roasting meat. From inside buildings and in dark areas of shadow under the great facades came the nasal reeling of flutes and sitars that softened voracious haggling in strange tongues.

And hiding in among the crowd, dark eyes regarded the three travelers malevolently.

One set of eyes regarded them differently and the man those eyes belonged to ran up to the three and proposed them hiring him as a guide and interpreter. Kaisa and Thorbjorn took him up on his offer, not eager to be at a disadvantage in Al-Zar. He introduced himself as Yusef Al-Amman and gathering from his attempt at describing his position and employment, they guessed he was slightly above a beggar in status. He was older than Styrkar and herself, but younger than Thorbjorn by a few years, Kaisa guessed, and was unkempt in his hair and hygiene. His clothes were in ill-repair, although not thread bare or moth eaten, and he kept his right hand tucked in the folds of his robes. He was harmless enough, however, and invited his newfound honored guests to eat at his home.

Not wishing to insult their interpreter and guide, they took him up on his offer and, that evening, sat down to a surprisingly vast meal of lamb, couscous, and dates and assorted other foods of the desert. Yusef Al-Amman also had a large family, comprising of several wives, who kept themselves in finer silks and gold than their husband, and his thirty three children. It was then also that Kaisa, Thorbjorn and Styrkar saw that his right hand was missing. He never spoke of it to them and they never asked him about it, but it was fairly obvious the reason for its removal. Al-Zar and the other desert lands did not tolerate many things and death and mutilation awaited those who ran afoul of the laws of these lands.

They spent the night in Yusef Al-Amman's home. It was that night that those who possessed the malevolent eyes came to the house as merchants claiming to be in need of a place to stay for the evening. Their host let them in with a smile and, once in the door,

threw off their disguises and attacked Yusef, his family and the three visitors with

scimitars. Styrkar, Kaisa and Thorbjorn handled them with surprising ease, slaughtering

them quickly and sending streams of blood flowing down the stairs and puddling on the

floors of Yusef Al-Amman's house. But not before they had killed Yusef Al-Amman and

several of his wives and children.

Searching the assassins, Styrkar discovered upon them rings that matched those of the

spy he had killed days before. It became clear now that certain of the desert folks were

conspiring against them, although for what reason they could not guess and they could

not fathom how people many miles away from Aardsberg and Tuska could know that

they were here.

They took their chances the next day, buying supplies to go into the desert without a

guide or a translator. Most of the merchants would only do business with Styrkar or

Thorbjorn and some even glared at Kaisa. One, however, did not. As they passed by an

awning under which a female merchant with her face completely veiled sat selling

strange ancient relics, she spoke to them by name.

They asked her how she knew their names and she told them that they would not

understand, adding as she fixed her eyes on Styrkar at least not yet. Forces knew that

Styrkar and Kaisa sought out the relic in the ancient ruined city of Al-Ghazan for the

great demon lord Baat'zaar. They knew Styrkar's mother was one of the people from the

Forbidden Lands beyond the Nordlands and that the only people who could use the

artifact would be of that race that lived in the days it was created, when all the lands were

cold and ice. Styrkar faced a challenge-either Baat'zaar would enslave him and use him and the artifact against men or Styrkar would fight Baat'zaar and destroy him. There was, however, an overwhelming force in the young Nordman-revenge. Revenge was driving Styrkar to become more powerful and it would drive him right into the claws of the demon lord if it were not brought under control. She told Styrkar that revenge in time would be his, but he had to be patient. He had to learn his powers. Many foes would lie at his feet, but only if he broke his deal with Baat'zaar and denied the demon lord the relic.

Then she spoke of Al-Ghazan in the middle of the sun glared pale sands of the Wastes. It has only been in recent times since the intolerant desert ones ruled the lands that it has been come to be called Al-Ghazan, for it was built in the days before all other races came to be and was called by another name long since forgotten. It was an unholy place and it was there the ancient Children of Ice hid the artifact. She refused to describe the artifact or what it could do, but warned them that only Styrkar must handle it, for he was of the blood of the Ancients and any others would perish horribly.

After that, she said no more and stepped back into the shadows of her awnings and the three realized that ears that were not supposed to hear about Styrkar and Al-Ghazan were near. They hastened off into the crowd.

They quickly gathered their supplies and headed into the desert searching for Al-Ghazan that night in hopes of preventing another assassination attempt. Again, they traveled by night and slept during the day. And again, the desert, once the three were two days out, turned into that dreary sameness that Styrkar and Kaisa had experienced several weeks before in the red deserts of that mysterious land of Baat'zaar.

Nothing occurred for five days, but on the morning of the fifth as the sun peeked over the horizon and threatened to cast its dry oppression upon the land and all on it, they spied the empty, crumbling towers of Al-Ghazan. It did not look like the architecture of

the desert folks with their domes and spires, nor did it look like the heavy castles of the

north built of somber rock. They drove their horses on, eager to make the ruined city that

spoke of untold ages.

The sun had started its dreaded arc and was almost halfway through its journey when

they reached the massive, dark ruins of windowless buildings next to crags and tors of the

same stone. They were unlike any buildings the three had seen before. They found a

small shell of building and decided to set up camp within and start their search the

following night.

There were many of the plain, dark buildings, so they started in the largest of ruins-the

towers. Several of them still rose up to the sky and Kaisa and Thorbjorn surmised that if

the artifact remained, it would be in them. Styrkar felt differently, though. He felt that the

Ancient Ones would not hide their artifacts in things that stood out on the horizon, where

any thief could find it, but that it was someplace more hidden from view. He looked at

the dark tors nearby and, while his companions climbed up the tallest of the towers, he

went to those jagged rocks.

Carved in the far side, away from the view of the dead city, Styrkar found a doorway

with a shallow portico. There were pillars, but they bore no ornamentation, and a

doorway open to the vast desert. The sun stretched into the antechamber and he walked

in, his feet shuffling quietly on the sand covered stone floor.

The interior was different from the exterior-strict lack of ornamentation gave way to

walls carved in runes and reliefs of horrific things that roamed either the planet, the

Ancient's dreams or both and high, vaulted ceilings. No furniture remained from that time, for the dry desert air and the sun reached through the doorway had disintegrated all of it. At the opposite end of the chamber was another doorway, but this was closed by a great stone door covered in spirals of runes. He went to that door and pushed against it with his left hand and was startled when the door turned easily in on one side. He walked in and was surprised to find that it was dimly lit by orbs that floated in the air and glowed blue. In the middle of the room was a stone pedestal covered in writing and imagery much like that of the rest of the inside chambers and floating over it was the artifact, or at least what he had hoped was the artifact. It was a plain, unpolished stone disc with a hole in the center.

As he looked at the disc floating upon its pedestal, a thin, pale woman taller than the towering Styrkar approached him and acknowledged him by name, telling him she had expected him. She also knew he came for the artifact for the demon Baat'zaar, who had promised the young Nordman revenge against Arnkell and Astrid's murderers. She explained that Baat'zaar has been requesting the artifact for some time, but has never found it, for only the Ancients know of the location and only those of the Ancients' blood can touch it. Baat'zaar knew of these, but sought it anyway, hoping for the opportunity for one with the blood of the Ancients to come into his clutches.

His minion Aethelwulf accidentally handed that opportunity to him when he killed Styrkar's parents and put one with the blood of the Ancients on the path of revenge. Baat'zaar jumped at the opportunity.

She then said that the thing on the pedestal was not the artifact, but a ruse to deceive Baat'zaar should he ever find this place, for while the knowledge of the artifact crept through the legends of the world, no one knew what it truly looked like. Although she knew that Styrkar had made a deal with Baat'zaar and was at risk for falling into the demon lord's servitude, she decided to show him the artifact itself. She put her hands over his eyes so should Baat'zaar have placed an enchantment upon him to find out where the artifact is, he could not do it through Styrkar's eyes. Her touch blinded him, but she told him to not panic, that she would give his sight back to him once she took him to the artifact and again after he was set free.

She guided him through what must have been a labyrinth, her warm, delicate hands touching his. The place was oddly cold for it being in a desert and Styrkar started shivering.

When she returned his sight, he was in a chamber that glowed blue and whose walls were covered in a thin layer of ice. Another carved pedestal was in the middle of the room and upon it floated the true artifact.

The real artifact was a highly polished orb that flowed of green and gold within. The woman then revealed to him what it was-the orb contained the essence of the world-the sap of the two magical trees long ago that existed when the world was cold and icy and before mortal men sought the places of the gods. The trees were known throughout the lands and in various faiths as the Trees of Life and Wisdom. Aeons ago, the trees were killed in a battle between Darfos and his master, the Dead God Abbath.

An oracle had foreseen their destruction and the Ancients were wise to take sap from those trees, for the Trees of Life and Wisdom bore no seeds. The Ancients put the saps into an orb of glass created from primordial sand and through religious ritual made it so none but the Ancients and their kind could touch it. The sap of the Trees was the life blood of the world and those who had the orb could harness the powers of the sap within.

It was unfortunate that the Ancient Ones of this city died before they could spirit the orb off to the colder northern lands. And the only way for Baat'zaar to obtain the orb and to use it was to enslave one of the blood of the Ancients.

Baat'zaar would let Styrkar have his revenge on Aethelwulf only after Styrkar was no longer needed to handle the artifact. While Aethelwulf was more a burden than a benefit, that deal made his existence far more valuable.

She then took Styrkar's hands and placed them on the orb and told him he now possessed the artifact and before him laid two choices. The first was to honor his deal with Baat'zaar and to give him the orb in return for serving the demon lord until he decided to fulfill his end of the bargain and let him kill Aethelwulf. The other was to take it into those frozen lands beyond the Nordlands and climb alone to the top of the tallest mountain where the gods hid and leave it there for them to receive it.

When Styrkar inquired as to why she did not take the orb herself to the north, she smiled and told him that, while she could guard the artifact, she was merely a guardian, not an Ancient One, and could not handle the orb. He put the orb into a belt pouch, creating a bulge, and the guardian blinded him again to escort him out.

Waiting in the chamber with the decoy artifact, however, were two of the white veiled things of Baat'zaar, who grabbed the blinded Styrkar and, before the guardian could act, gated away with him to their white galley. No longer bound to the ruins, she ran out to find Styrkar's companions that she knew he had come with.

Styrkar this time was bound to the mast of the great ship, his face against the unholy white wood and shirtless, and was brutally flogged by one of Baat'zaar's creatures. For the rest of the journey, he was to be beaten five times every day and the one with the whip would get a shot in on him every time it passed him. He was not fed and given just enough water to keep him alive. This lasted for several scorching days until the ship returned to the city in the Abyss and Styrkar was freed from the mast, shackled and guided unceremoniously down the gangplank to the wharf.

Baat'zaar awaited him there and laughed when the trembling, blind Nordman was shoved to the ground before him, for now he had the orb and he had Styrkar.

As the demon lord prepared for his campaign, Styrkar was thrown into a pit with a metal grate on top, not that he could see to escape. It was very narrow, preventing him from moving in the slightest.

Kaisa and Thorbjorn, along with the guardian, raced back to Al-Zar and from there, returned through the Grey Mountains to Takros, where they caught a ship back to Tuska. One of the galleys had arrived in Tuska just prior to the return of Kaisa and Thorbjorn. Upon receiving the news of Styrkar's abduction and that he had the artifact needed by the demon, Kjell ordered the ship confiscated. The city's militia stormed the vessel, successfully taking the blasphemous ship, but not its insidious crew, for they had fought to every last man.

Curious to finally view the faces of these men, Kjell ordered for one to have his robes and shrouds removed and everyone on that deck jumped back in horror at what they saw. Only the eyes were close to being human. The mouth was wide and full of metallic, sharp teeth. The body was full of short, black fur and the body was covered in arms sewn to it from the victims that it had eaten on the voyages between the Tuska and the Abyss. There were four legs with sharp cloven hooves and the thing reeked of rotting corpses, a stench that the perfumed robes had covered up.

The white galley confiscated, they searched the horrid thing and saw with their own eyes what Styrkar and Kaisa had reported seeing. Kjell would have burned the thing as it was anchored in port had it not been that it was needed to travel to Baat'zaar's land in the Abyss to rescue Styrkar and the orb. The supernatural guardian of the orb knew how to start Baat'zaar's galleys and knew that, if left alone, they would sail back to the hellish port city in his plane, for the ships were enchanted to always return to the Abyss and to that city, no matter where his minions took them.

But Baat'zaar was already on his way with his ships and troops and with Styrkar. Blind and his hands bound before him, the Nordman was made to rest on his knees next to the demon lord under the awning on the deck. He was in a great deal of pain, with gashes from the whips on his back and arms and chest. Sooner or later, the ships will stop and Styrkar would be expected to use that orb to harness the life powers of the Trees and make Baat'zaar invincible, but he had no idea how that was to happen.

A thought entered his head and it was a risky one that might mean his death, but anything now was better than being a slave to the demon responsible for killing his parents. He could not see the sides of the ship, but he threw himself to one side, running as fast as he could. There was a commotion of voices and Baat'zaar shouting things in his infernal language. Hands grabbed at his long, blonde hair and his pants, but he swung wildly or kicked and kept scrambling until finally he felt a huge furry paw grasp him firmly by the back of the neck and slam him face down on the deck. Styrkar squirmed and wriggled about in an attempt to get free. The hand was joined by others that grabbed his legs and at first, he thought it was all over. He gave one last desperate kick and broke one leg free of the hands and made contact with something he did not like the feel of even remotely. He started fighting again and felt himself bump against a railing, voices called out in words he could not understand, and he felt himself somehow break free. There was a whistling breeze sound in his ears and his insides felt as if they were floating. He was falling.

The impact was extremely painful. It stung horribly and the force of hitting the surface of the briny sea was like hitting rock.

Baat'zaar was furious and ordered the ships to turn around. However, their great size kept them from making the turns in a timely fashion and, by the time they returned to the area he had fallen overboard, Styrkar and the artifact were lost, gone out of sight to the depths below.

Below the waters, Styrkar held his breath as he sank far below the waves. He dreaded the thought of drowning, for he had seen how men flailed about and fought for air as their lungs filled up. After a little over a minute, he resigned himself to a painful fate and drew in his first breath since hitting the water. Much to his surprise, he drew in air. He was breathing underwater. He remembered the orb and that the guardian told him it had the life force of the world.

At first, he feared being blind, but the orb gradually dispelled the blindness and he realized he was in an ocean upon his own planet. He had heard of ruins of cities under the sea and that some were very ancient, dating back to the world's first civilization, even older than the Ancient Ones he had descended from. This was one of them. They were as large as the basalt towers of the desert and larger than the pyramids and ruins he had seen in the Abyss. He roamed the white sand covered streets and looked into lichen encrusted window sills, but most of the architectural details and the interiors were completely overtaken by coral and other sea life. The orb in his pouch fed and healed his wounds

from Baat'zaar's torture both on the seas and in his dungeon.

As he wandered through the ruins, a voice from within a small building spoke to him,

calling him by name. When he asked how the unseen being knew of him and how others

knew to call him by name, the voice answered that all of the supernatural know each

other and that it was familiar with the Children of the Ice in particular. It also said that it

knew Astrid very well and he mourned the day she had been murdered by Aethelwulf.

It then told Styrkar of these ruins-how long before even the world was cold and ocean

flooded this area of the world there were the First Ones who lived when the seas and

lands were in different places than they are now. It was they who originally planted the

Trees that other civilizations held sacred up until the end of the reign of the Children of

the Ice, when the orb Styrkar held was created at their death.

The orb, as Styrkar knew, was the sap of those trees since they were said not to have

seed. The life essence had been preserved, but the voice then told him that this orb had a

place-that the ruins he found it in were to protect it from Baat'zaar, who was back in

those days not even half as powerful as he is now. Baat'zaar has always sought to rule the

planes and the reason he chose this world Terrascape as his main objective was that for

some reason, all the planes converged here. It was a hub for planar travel and if Baat'zaar

could control this world, he could control any other world in any other plane.

Styrkar, it went on, was now the only one not in the Forbidden Lands above the

Nordlands who had the power to stop him. And Baat'zaar knew Styrkar had not yet

reached his fullest powers and would continually try to enslave him until he was of enough power to take on Baat'zaar alone. Time was not on Baat'zaar's side anymore, as the plunge overboard with the orb has thrown the demon lord's plans off considerably.

And then the speaker let itself be known-coming out of the house was a large, blue crab-like creature upon which sat a shell of glimmering blues and silvers and bearing upon the top three horn-like bells. Styrkar knew him immediately as the Sea Lord that his mother spoke of very fondly in tales. With his great pinchers, the Sea Lord cut the ropes on Styrkar's hands and then spoke again to him and warned him about controlling his feelings, especially when concerning his anger and desire for vengeance. It was that which made him easy prey for the demon lord. Revenge, he echoed previous advisors, would be Styrkar's in time if he was patient and took the time to have the power to follow it through.

Upon finishing his conversation, he told the Nordman to climb upon his great shell and he carried him many miles to the shore not far from Takros, for if he reappeared in Tuska, the demon lord would know and seek him out again.

When Kaisa, Kjell and Thorbjorn saw the fleet of white ships, they drew weapons, hoping that if the demon lord attacked, they would be able to take many demons with them before succumbing. They were surprised when he moved in within earshot and hailed them. He announced that Styrkar had died escaping on his way to the war, falling over the side of the ship. Kaisa felt as if her heart had just been torn out when he uttered the words. She felt very little relief hearing he had "temporarily" set Baat'zaar's plans by taking the orb to his watery grave. The demon laughed and turned his ships back to the Abyss in order to figure out how to fetch the orb from the ocean floor and how to use it without getting destroyed by it.

Numbness found its way into every vessel and cell of her body over the news Styrkar's demise. Kaisa fell into a deep depression, not talking to anyone and sitting for hours crying. She missed his fiery, blue eyes and long blonde hair and the way he softly stuttered in his heavy accent. Upon their return to Tuska, Kaisa had made up her mind and renounced the Order of the Blue Tygers. Thorbjorn feared for her and tried to convince her to reconsider, that Styrkar would have wanted her to go on being a paladin, but his concerns fell on deaf ears. She took Styrkar's belongings-his weapons and his armor and his horse-along with hers and fled from the city. She did not return to Aardsberg. She simply vanished, although Thorbjorn had guessed she had run off someplace to mourn her lover.

In Takros, Styrkar was back on square one with his life after the death of his parents. With very little money and no weapons, having left them in the ruins on his horse, with exception to his long sword, which Baat'zaar now held in his armories, he was pretty much a beggar until someone, a merchant heading north, recognized him as the adventurer who passed through several weeks before with the lady paladin and offered him a job as an escort for a caravan. The Nordman accepted and within days was on his way back to more familiar lands.

Kaisa would not be waiting for him. Having turned her back on her order, she rode across the border in hopes of fulfilling for Styrkar what he had not been able to do in life-kill Aethelwulf. She joined Aethelwulf's legions as a mercenary, hoping to infiltrate his keep and murder him, knowing full well that she would never escape alive. His guards would surely fall upon her as she was hacking him to pieces and kill her where she stood, but she could not bear losing Styrkar.

Her presence did not go unnoticed, for those mercenaries who had had run-ins with Aardsberg's paladins in the past identified her readily and exposed her as a spy to their officers. She was brought before Aethelwulf with the great sword of Arnkell, which had been taken from her by her captors.

Aethelwulf was not as she expected. He looked youthful for his years and had long, hair and a full, straight haired beard. He was as tall as Styrkar, possibly taller, and had a possessed, baleful look in his dark eyes. No crown sat upon his head, for as she would later learn he reserved crowns for when he conquered nations. He also wore no garish, fancy clothes, a manner she had also noticed in Styrkar and attributed to their Nordman culture.

He recognized the sword and questioned her angrily about from where it came and how she came about it. She told him it had belonged to Styrkar, son of Arnkell Dark Horse and Astrid and who sought to kill Aethelwulf. The king laughed deeply and ridiculed Styrkar for sending a woman in his stead. Kaisa dourly answered through her teeth that Arnkell's son had perished in the sea and that she had chosen to carry out his revenge.

One of the king's advisors told him to have her beheaded here in the throne room and her head sent to Aardsberg as a warning, but Aethelwulf had other plans. He needed someone intimate with Aardsberg's defenses, especially concerning the Order of the Blue Tygers. He was also aware that, being so tied to Styrkar and still yet a paladin, she would not provide this assistance willingly. So he sent her to the dungeons and told his chief interrogator that he only had to deny her sleep until Aethelwulf said otherwise.

So Kaisa was forced to stay awake for the better part of five days, the guards taking shifts with her. Aethelwulf checked in on her from time to time and, on the fifth day when her hallucinations and headache had become too unbearable for her, he brought in the clerics who served the arch devil Darfos and sorcerers to cast enchantments and bindings upon her while her resistance and will were undermined.

They put upon her, too, a secret quest; for Darfos had his own plans and spoke to those in his inner circle of priests of them. The arch devil was not happy with his demon minion's behavior, for he knew that he would soon have enough power to attempt to usurp him, and he ordered his priests to seek out a paladin, one whose fall from grace would be easy to arrange, for no paladin would willingly serve him otherwise. This he needed because in his early days, prior to achieving his stature in the Abyss, he foolishly put protective enchantments on those who sided with him in his war with another devil so that creature could not destroy them. It never occurred to him at the time that those permanent protections would stop him from defending himself against Baat'zaar.

The priests were ordered to go along with Baat'zaar and Aethelwulf until there came a crucial time where the paladin could take advantage of the situation and kill the demon lord and the vile king. Then Darfos would take the lands and worlds that the two had captured for his own.

Kaisa was finally allowed to sleep and she fell into a restless, violent dream world more vivid than she had ever dreamed before. When she awoke, it hit her that she was now bound to those who she swore to both her order and Styrkar to destroy. She plummeted into a deep, heavy depression that seemed to grasp her heart and suffocated her. Once bound by the priests to serve against her will, Aethelwulf, still not fully trusting of her, kept her within his sight at all times, keeping her in his throne room when awake and in a cage he installed in his chambers at night.

As Styrkar traveled with the caravan to Tuska, a force of raiders from Aethelwulf's army ambushed them. Aethelwulf had assigned certain troops to disrupt trade routes and leading this particular bunch of raiders, as the Fates would have it, was a face familiar to the Nordman, although he had only recalled that face in his head for the better part of the last three years. The last time Styrkar had seen the sergeant barking out orders, however, he had torch in hand and was setting fire to the homes of the defenders of a certain village in the eastern parts of Fantoft and ordering his soldiers to kill everyone there. Styrkar decided it was time to return the favor. He cut through the raiders with extreme prejudice as he made a beeline to his foe. By the time he reached him, the young Nordman was covered in gore and had blood dripping from his battle axe.

The very sight of him caused the sergeant to gasp and with wide-eyed fear he realized who this caravan guard was, even before Styrkar invoked his father's name in a war cry. He fought against the bloodied Horseman's crashing blows until his sword was sent flying from him. The sergeant pleaded for mercy, but Styrkar would have none of that. He hacked the man as he screamed his death throes and lopped his head off in angry strokes.

Of the others, he left one alive despite the words of the other guards that they would be spared and taken to justice and despite several of the guards, men from Murtha, protesting loudly against Styrkar's furious slaughter. With the blood of the dead raiders Styrkar wrote a note in his left handed scrawl and it said "*I live*". He put the head in a sack and told the messenger to take the head and note to Aethelwulf under the threat that failure would bring the maniacal Nordman upon him to inflict a slow, painful death. The man fled in fear with the sack.

Styrkar then turned his attention to his foe's possessions. He searched for and found the sergeant's long sword, which burned with a blue flame and felt cold to the touch. He also took the dead sergeant's warhorse, a beautiful golden brown warhorse with a mane and tail as white as the ice of the Nordlands. And without conscience, he convinced the others to not bury the bodies of the raiders and let the remains serve as warning to other bandits, but he reveled in his soul at denying the men proper burial and allowing dogs and foul birds to feed upon them.

As the caravan rode on, Styrkar searched the sergeant's saddlebags. Among his things he found a journal and he read it, finding entries describing the attacks on the villages of the Fantoft and Stromgald Horsemen and names of those involved and he grinned broadly.

As Styrkar battled more raiding parties, although none with any more of those he sought vengeance against, and made his way with the caravan to Tuska, the messenger arrived at the court of Aethelwulf with the items from the Nordman. The king had him butchered for failing on his mission and coming back alive. He then read the note signed by the "Son of Arnkell", which Kaisa got an accidental glimpse of and felt a glimmer of hope in her despair. When the king went to look in the bloody sack, the head fell out of the bottom and rolled out before the throne for all to see and gasps of horror and fearful whispers filled the chamber.

Aethelwulf looked at it in barely concealed fear. He did not like this sergeant-for the man was insolent and was assigned to lead raiding parties as part of his punishment for stirring up the ire of the king. It was the fact that Styrkar lived and announced it with the brutal death of one of Aethelwulf's men, though it did not occur to him at the time why that particular man.

Nonetheless, Styrkar's vengeance had begun.

Aethelwulf decided that if Styrkar would mete out vengeance in such vile, horrific ways, he would have to do it with the one he loved. Kaisa would ride out and do battle with him whether she liked it or not when the time came and he told her that she would be made to kill Styrkar. And he sent out his spies to seek out wherever the Son of Arnkell may be.

When the caravan arrived in Tuska, Styrkar searched for Kaisa and Thorbjorn. He found his fellow Nordman with other Horsemen assembled in a tavern and was told that they were gathering to take on the armies of Aethelwulf, for the king's armies were moving against Murtha, to the west of Aardsberg. While Murtha and its whiney, weak men were of no real concern to the Horsemen, they had to stop Stromgald from getting a foothold within the nation.

Thorbjorn also told him of Kaisa's departure and that he suspected it was to carry out Styrkar's vengeance against Aethelwulf. The burly Nordman feared for her as nothing had been heard concerning her from anywhere and she had left in a deep and heavy mood that even penetrated her soul. This troubled Styrkar as well, for he cared deeply for her and dreaded the thought of anything happening to her.

The next day, the Horsemen set out for Murtha, although they were but a pale shadow of their former selves, in days when Arnkell raised his sword and let forth a battle cry that put fear into the hearts of their foes. It was a three day ride to Murtha by horse and the siege had begun by the time they got there. It was barely a battle, really-more of the men of Murtha hiding behind the battlements and shouting rude names down at the overwhelming army outside the castle walls, for no man in Murtha would actually pick up a sword and, while the women were more assertive, they spent most of their time bitching at the men. So it was up to the Horsemen alone to take on the army-one hundred and fifty against five thousand.

Thorbjorn blew the Horn of Fantoft, the land west of Stromgald where the bravest of Horsemen dwelled, and they charged into battle. They were not expected and some of the men of Stromgald broke ranks at the sight of the legendary Horsemen. Despite their small numbers, they tore into the ranks and sent blood and body parts to every end of the battlefield and trampling hapless infantrymen that ran before them. A lieutenant yelled out orders in an effort to get his men under control and again, Styrkar recognized the face as one of the raiders who torched his village and the villages of the others and he bore down upon him. There were screams as the man was put cruelly to the axe and Styrkar dismounted and hacked off his head.

And then Styrkar noticed the bigger prize-the commander of the battle was Aethelwulf's youngest son, mentioned by name in the journal as "Bardo". The frantic Nordman marked the body of the lieutenant with a lance impaling it to the ground and jumped onto his palomino warhorse to kill Bardo. The two clashed, fighting on horseback until Bardo fell from his mount and then the two took to cleaving at each other on foot. Styrkar had learned a new trick in battle; he swept at the prince's spindly legs with his axe in a way that knocked the prince to the ground. Once down, Bardo was butchered and beheaded in a most gruesome fashion.

With their prince killed, the forces of Stromgald fled into the mountains.

Of the others captured, Styrkar left only one alive despite the words of other Horsemen that they would be spared and despite several of the men from Murtha protesting loudly against Styrkar's furious slaughter. With the blood of the dead raiders Styrkar wrote a note in his left handed scrawl and it said *"You will join them soon"*. He put the heads in a sack and told the messenger to take the heads and note to Aethelwulf under the threat that failure would bring the maniacal Nordman upon him to inflict a slow, painful death. The man fled in fear with the sack.

Styrkar then turned his attention to his foe's possessions. He took the dead prince's warhorse, a beautiful creature as black as the long winter skies of the Nordlands, as well as the sergeant's battle axe, which burned with red fire and felt warm to the touch. He took the prince's armor made of the hides of black dragons and his long sword of a sinister red glow and the silver ring that resembled an ouroborous. And without conscience, he convinced the others to not bury the bodies of the raiders as he reveled in his soul at denying the men proper burial and allowing dogs and foul birds to feed upon them. Except for the body of Bardo, which he burned on a funeral pyre and requested a metal flask and when the fire burned out, Styrkar put the ashes of Aethelwulf's son in that metal flask as a final trophy.

The sword Styrkar gave Bardo's sword to Thorbjorn as a souvenir and, after searching the bodies and battlefield for war trophies, the Horsemen rallied around the two and cheered on the Son of Arnkell, their new leader Thorbjorn and swore further vengeance against Aethelwulf.

The Nordmen did not stay in Murtha for long. Once having taken what they wanted from their fallen foes and burning their dead on pyres, they fled from this place of womanly men and manly women. Both sides were elated that the Nordmen went back to their transplanted home of Tuska. The Horsemen got tired of the people of Murtha screaming insults at them about needless killing and murdering the "children" of Stromgald, even though most of the enemy dead were the same ages as the men of Fantoft, for the Nordlanders were raised to be warriors from birth. Once their defenders had rode off for Tuska, the people of Murtha set to burying the dead of Stromgald with honors and, although in agreement that the atrocities committed by the Horsemen must be condemned, there was debate on whether censure was appropriate or would a resolution demanding the displaced Nordmen pay reparations to the families of the Stromgald battle dead be a more forceful response.

They were wise enough not to desecrate the graveyard left by the Riders of Fantoft, lest they pass this way and discover the deed. Even without organization and a homeland, they were more than a match for the barely existent Murtha militia.

The one hundred or so surviving Horsemen rode into Tuska triumphantly and told Kjell what had occurred on the battlefield. He was ecstatic over the news of Bardo's death and laughed about Styrkar's method of breaking the news to Aethelwulf. The city of Tuska rejoiced the victory for the better part of a week and from refugee camps around the walls of the city came more Horsemen and volunteers to join them.

In Stromgald and the subjugated Nordlands, however, Aethelwulf mourned for the better part of a week. The king was furious and vowed revenge upon Styrkar, swearing he would have the Son of Arnkell's head on a pole over the city's gates. Bardo's mother, however, could not take the loss of her child and by the end of the week, became so overtaken by despair that she poisoned herself. So full of rage was Aethelwulf that he sent his middle and favorite son, Vegard, to seek and destroy Styrkar.

For Kaisa, however, hope burned stronger. She knew now Styrkar had not died and was coming for Aethelwulf.

Styrkar did not celebrate for long, however, and rode off for the Nordlands and that mysterious land of ice that his mother had come from. He decided that the orb belonged there, in the hands of the Gods upon the tallest mountain where it would be forever out of the hands of men. And there was something else-his father's sword and his weapons from the pyramid were in the hands of his foe Aethelwulf. He was not sure, too, of Kaisa's fate and had to learn if she was still alive.

He rode upon Bardo's horse and took along two others-his own steed and that of the sergeant he killed-so he could travel with fewer stops to rest. He did not tell Thorbjorn or Kjell where he was going, but that he had to go and go alone.

The path he traveled took him again to the Spectre Wood and it was at its horrid edge that he camped that night. His dreams were vivid and violent, a vision of perpetual twilight in a frigid place of dark ice, where the great folk of his mother dwelled. He saw himself ascending a treacherous peak that went up into the clouds beyond even the sight of men and in one hand he clutched the orb in bloodied fingers, torn raw from the rocks. The cold air tore into him and the winds threatened to whip him off of the mountain, but he clung on and clambered up the black, primordial rock face. Upon reaching the summit, he did not see the gods he expected, but the most horrific entities he ever laid eyes on-crawling, evil, massive things that protected the gods of men. He saw, too, the Spectre Wood when there was a city of white was there and in the center were two Trees-an oak and a pine-that glowed with divine energy.

Something woke him from his dream before he could enter the city, as if the gods had showed him too much and realized their mistake. He knew now, though, that the Spectre

Wood, or what was once where the Spectre Wood now stood, and the land beyond the Nordlands were connected somehow.

After eating his breakfast of dried venison, Styrkar set off into the forest, hoping that he would be able to travel through the worst places by day and avoid the ghostly visages he had seen on his last journey when he and Kaisa and Thorbjorn had traveled to Tuska. Even in the bright of day, voices whispered to him from supernatural things and shadows moved about in the corner of his eyes.

But something was different about this journey, for Styrkar had to travel a slightly different route to get to Stromgald's border. He passed closer to the core of the place than he was comfortable with and came upon a ruin of an old tower that the ancient trees had blocked from view from beyond the forest's edge. Or maybe it had been blocked by supernatural means. Against his better judgment, he stopped at it, tying his horses to a decaying tree stump.

The tower's base indicated that what was left was not the entire edifice and that it had been of a size greater than any tower he had seen, except for possibly the ones of the desert. Unlike Thorbjorn and Kaisa, he logged nothing of what he saw in the carvings or its location, although later he would log that he had come upon a dark tower of unknown origin. He did not feel right about the ruins of the civilizations the preceded men and felt that the less that was known of them, the better. A memory of Astrid came to him-when he was a child, she had told him stories on rare occasion about towers that were as black as ash and had no windows and how it was merciful that those things that dwelled within them had died long before man came along. She told him that they did not belong here and that they controlled the storms when they came and that she had heard from her people that they did not die off, but that they went under the world and became the foul

demons and devils below. Astrid also warned him to stay away from those towers, but

now the towers were of importance and entirely unavoidable.

He walked into the tower to find stairs going both up into the heights and down into

darkness. Knowing the great tower had collapsed most of the way, he chose to go down.

At the bottom was a hall that was wide and reached into dark heights above. Debris of the

gradually failing vaults covered sections of the strange, octagon-tiled floor, but it was the

doorway to a room ahead that Styrkar had interest in, for Astrid told him, too, of the great

knowledge the oldest of the world's inhabitants and perhaps there was something he felt

could use hidden in these ruins.

Dusty footprints in the debris were clearer near the door and, in his torchlight; he spotted

something just inside the threshold. It was the skeletal, mummified remains of an

adventurer of some sort. No cause of death could be discerned by Styrkar as he took the

stained backpack off of the pathetic, small body and searched through it. He found,

among personal effects, a journal and read it to see what, if any, information concerning

his quest it could give him.

In the journal, it described a party's venturing into the dreaded center of the forest.

Apparently, rumors abounded in the newer kingdoms of the south of riches untold buried

in the forest and such greed led many, including this person and her friends, to trespass

upon it. The first few pages described the excitement of looking for enough wealth for

her and her friends to live "like royalty forever". These dreams crumbled slowly with

each writing of each day until the last desperate one she had written in these ancient, unholy halls. The first thing the book did was confirm Kaisa's fear about the things that looked like moss covered tree branches, which Styrkar found quite disturbing as well.

The second was the book described seven places within the area most avoided by the wiser of men. The first, which told of the group entering nears the coast, was of a swamp with dead bodies of warriors seen in its murky pools of water. The second was the ruins of a great city of marble buildings, although the color of those buildings had been obscured by dirt and mold and age. Within that city was the third. In the center of the city were two tree trunks of unbelievable size and one of those trunks had a brown and dark green petrified resin that the author and her deceased companions felt would be of some value to those of the rest of the coast. In her backpack, Styrkar found a sack of dull brown and dark green things that looked more like smooth rocks than bits of resin. The fourth was a cemetery, although not the one Styrkar and his friends had found earlier, and in it was a crypt. The author believed that a dreadful bunch of people had been buried there and had lost two of her friends to things within, although she was too upset to mention what those things were or the manner in which the hapless members of her group died. The fifth was a circle of strange stones of a size that no mortal creatures could have moved into the forest from the mountains. The sixth was of a place where some of the bloodiest fighting of the battle had taken place where no trees or brush grew and no animals, not even the birds and insects came. Even the very spirits that roamed the forest acting out for eternity their moments of glory and death did not venture to such a place. The seventh was this tower, where she sought shelter from something in the forest that she could not describe.

Styrkar went back up the stairs and brought his horses within the tower and decided to stay in the ruins, no matter how haunted or cursed, for the night. According to her descriptions, nothing outside seemed to venture into these ruins, but she had felt that they held a far greater evil than anything lurking outside, save the crypt, the blasted area and that stone circle. He returned to the body and continued reading by torchlight.

She mentioned, too, a gypsy who lurked the forest in a caravan wagon and who had, at the beginning of the group's trespass upon the Spectre Wood, warned them of evils within the forest and that what they sought was not worth venturing into the core of the forest to the most cursed and forgotten sites there. She added that the woman said her name was Desdinova and, when pressed by the adventurers, confessed that she, and only she, could live in this forest. She never explained how that was possible, but Styrkar suspected she was some kind of supernatural guardian.

He took the journal for further reading on his travels and continued his search of the ruins. There was a great arch and a room beyond. Styrkar entered and found most of it had caved in, but by the twisted metal shelves and the scattering of a large, pale, vellum-like paper that this was a library or archive of some sort. He picked up some of the dusty pages, but the writing was a complicated series of glyphs that he could not translate. Nevertheless, he collected up as many as he could and tucked them into the journal, careful to not cause the fragile sheets to crumble from their countless aeons of age. This was the only place he could explore, for the tunnel had caved in some distance beyond. He returned to his horses and slept in the entrance of the tower until the next day. When he awoke, he rode as quickly as he could through the Spectre Wood until he reached those areas where the trees were not bulbous and twisted and the visages that haunted the battlefields and ancient ruins did not dwell. By the end of the next day, he

was far from the haunted forest and into the foothills of the mountains of the Nordlands.

He stopped at a small village and in the morning, he started his journey into Stromgald.

He entered the Royal Forest early the next morning and fate smiled favorably upon him

that day, for by chance, Aethelwulf's eldest son and heir to the throne, Harwulf, was

hunting deer in the forest and came face to face with Styrkar. Harwulf recognized

Bardo's horse and tears welled in his eyes upon meeting for the first and only time his

brother's killer. Styrkar knew only that he was someone from the court of Aethelwulf, as

he was hunting in the good king's forest, and charged at him. Harwulf raised his bow and

shot off an arrow that skimmed across the Horseman's ear. It did not stop the incensed

charge and the prince barely had a chance to get sword out before being engaged by his

adversary. The two clashed ferociously, one bent on revenge of his brother and the other

of a desire to complete his quest without discovery by Aethelwulf. Styrkar, however,

proved the better fighter and drove his weapon through Harwulf's chest.

The rest of the hunting party had heard the battle and Styrkar could hear them coming as

he gathered up Harwulf's bow and quiver of arrows. He climbed upon the prince's black

horse and guided his other three horses away from the scene of the battle.

A great search went through the forest looking for the murderer of the prince and the

others figured that he was killed by bandits, for the tracks of several horses had been

discovered, but ended at a stream. Aethelwulf knew better. He knew Styrkar had come

and killed another of his children. This blow was more devastating to the king and he

became violently enraged. He killed the messenger of the news of Harwulf's death and,

after the national mourning of his son, close behind that of Bardo's death, he took Kaisa and Arnkell's sword and went out himself to hunt down Styrkar, despite Baat'zaar's orders for him to do otherwise. He warned the king that the Son of Arnkell was not coming after him, but was heading for the Forbidden Lands beyond the Nordlands. The demon lord's orders were ignored as Aethelwulf and Vegard, in two separate parties, sought out Styrkar in Stromgald and the southern lands, both laying waste to the villages and towns that were unlucky to lay in their paths.

Styrkar reached Fantoft without incident and recognized his immediately the mountains and valleys of his homeland. He sought out the village he had left years ago and found its ruins, though most of the bodies had been long since taken by beasts and by nature. The carved, tarred wood homes were gone and burned out shells and frames stood in their place. Although almost four years had passed, He found the blacksmith shop he was apprenticing at when the invasion occurred and set his camp up there. Before sleeping, he prayed to the deceased souls of the village, most importantly to his father and mother.

In his dreams, Astrid visited her son and told him where the mountain he sought was in the far reaches of the Forbidden Lands and that he had to be careful with the Others, the gods who protected the Old Gods. He was to find the great city of the Children of the Ice, the last place where his mother's people dwelled in the world and where Arnkell had met her and married her, and they would help him on his quest. Unlike most, Styrkar would be welcomed to those lands, as he was her son, and many would seek to aid him against Baat'zaar and Darfos. She then told him that she had wished she could have somehow prevented his part in all of this and that she had learned of it from a witch called Desdinova. When asked about the witch, Astrid confessed she did not know much about her except she was not of this world. However, she seemed neither good nor evil and, aside from her powers of clairvoyance, she knew nothing about from what plane she came from.

He left the ruins in the morning and, a few days later, reached the border of the Forbidden Lands. The sky had become darker the further north he had rode and now, even when the southern lands had a noonday sun, it was twilight here and streams of wavering light flowed across the skies like rivers. The mountains grew steeper and were covered in ice and snow that never melted. He found traveling more difficult, for now he could not just ride easily through valleys or along ridges, but had to twist and wind down troll trails. What took him half a day to ride now took over a day and without a regular rising and setting of the sun, he rested during those times he rode upon his own horse and not the three he took from his foes, for his horse had been trained to follow paths.

He finally came upon a great city where all the buildings were of glacier ice and that glowed blue under the dancing lights overhead. He knew right away as he looked upon the delicate glass-like spires and buildings carved with dragons that this was the city of the people of his mother and he rode with haste to it.

The people there knew immediately who he was and greeted him warmly despite his father being of the ignorant people of the south. They looked much like his mother with long, white hair and of tall stature and he was guided immediately to an elder called Wograven, who was considered among them the wisest.

Wograven lived in a tower in the center of the city and he had a long, flowing white mane and beard, but he did not look the aged scholar. He looked only slightly older than Styrkar, in fact, but he assured the Son of Astrid that he was older than most men could fathom, as was Astrid up until the day she was killed. They were of a race that did not age once they reached adulthood and that knew much because they lived before mere men took over the world and learned to sing their memories. They lived long when the Great Trees stood in what was called the Spectre Wood and near the ruins of no less than five previous civilizations of beings that predated those of current men. Styrkar told him of a dream he had in the Spectre Wood and of the tower and its ruined tunnel and of the first, Wograven spoke of the Trees and that Styrkar first had to take the orb to the mountain known as Hathan-ka in the north near the top of the world and present it to the Gods there. Then, he would have to go to the dreaded Spectre Wood and that that quest would have to do with the Great Trees, although he could not tell Styrkar what that quest might be.

Of the tower, he would not speak except to say it was from the oldest of all civilizations and that he must avoid those places in the future. Styrkar showed him the papers he had found and Wograven told him that if he wanted them translated, he would do so, and he would have them done after his quest to the great peak Hathan-ka, but that he might not want to know what they might mean.

Wograven also told him of a person who has been to Hathan-ka several times who could be a guide if he saw fit. Her name was Freya and she was a friend of Astrid's before she wed Arnkell and moved to the southern lands. Styrkar said he would welcome what help she could give him.

He was taken to her home by Wograven. Freya was a tall woman with white hair and eyes of ice blue. She remembered Astrid and spoke to Styrkar about his mother. She said she had been saddened by the news of her friend's death and feared for Styrkar's survival. Hearing of him winning a victory at Murtha was a big relief and she hoped he would be as great of a man as Arnkell had been in life.

They spoke of Styrkar's pending quest to Hathan-ka and of the orb. Freya repeated what he had heard of the orb and the Trees, but added that what many did not know is that the Trees produced one seed each and that those seeds were kept upon Hathan-ka. To get the seeds from the Gods, Styrkar would have to scale it alone and burn the resin of the Tree of Life to summon them to him. Once the Gods knew he was the one who had the orb, they would give him the seeds and tell him of what he must do with them. She could not say whether it would stop Darfos or Baat'zaar's attempt to gain control of the world, but it was something that had to be done in order to keep the demons from getting power that would make them unstoppable.

Styrkar and Freya took two of the horses, leaving the others in Wograven's royal stables with his great white horses, and rode north for the dark peaks at the top of the world, where the fabled Hathan-ka rose to untold heights.

While Styrkar carried out his journeys, the southern lands were in turmoil. Aethelwulf and Vegard's wraths had no limits and they were laying waste to the kingdoms that bordered Stromgald. Murtha was the first to fall; being the place Bardo had met his demise. The people of Murtha had rode out to Vegard, greeting him as a hero of Stromgald and offering gold and an apology for Bardo's death during the earlier invasion. Vegard responded by razing the city and murdering all within-men and women, old and children, healthy and sick. Rivers of blood ran in the streets as Murtha burned and its national treasures stripped and chopped apart for Vegard's hoard. The heads of Murtha's senators and ministers were impaled on metal poles around the city and Vegard sent messengers with the president and vice president's heads to Aardsberg and Tuska, demanding that Styrkar be turned over to King Aethelwulf, lest they face the destruction that had fell upon Murtha.

By now, however, the legend of Styrkar in his victory at Murtha had attracted enough of the Horsemen out of their hiding and brought forth volunteers, including paladins and rangers, eager to join the Horsemen in both cities and they rode out to take on Vegard and Aethelwulf's armies.

This time, Baat'zaar knew Styrkar was no longer in the Nordlands or the New Kingdoms and decided to let the king and his prince go to war in hopes Aardsberg and Tuska would be defeated and the conquest of the world thus furthered.

Thorbjorn led the Horsemen when they encountered Vegard and his forces at the Spectre Wood. It was in a place that was not part of the ancient battlefield, but was still thick with trees and they used those trees to ambush the prince and his men. Vegard was overwhelmed and killed, much as his father's minions had killed Arnkell, the hero of the Nordlands, and his head was sent by Thorbjorn's orders to Aethelwulf. The last surviving male heir to Aethelwulf's throne was now dead.

The head came to Aethelwulf's palace, but the king was not there as he was leading a search for Styrkar. His daughter, the Princess Arnfasta, however, received the head of her beloved, favorite brother and screamed and fell to her knees wailing in sorrow. She ordered for her father to be found and told of Vegard's killing by the Horsemen. It was more than she could handle, however, and that night, she plunged a poisoned dagger into her chest and died in horrific, agonizing seizures.

Styrkar and Freya traveled for the better part of a week to the mountains that sat upon the top of the world-The Sacred Peaks of Hazor. It was from these mountains that flowed the rivers that created the oceans and seas of Terrascape, including the Hardanger Sea that the Nordlands rose above and the Sea of Mystics that Tuska stood watch over so many miles and days in the south. They stood like jagged spines reaching into the sky that was forever twilight with the most intense and colorful of the dancing streams of light. Freya guided him over steep mountains and deep valleys to the beginning of the range of the foreboding crags, where they encountered the great black wolves that dwelled there and protected the mountains. Styrkar killed the pack that ambushed them, but saved two whelps which he would raise for his guardians and war dogs.

It took them over a day to get past the first peaks, Paza-ka and Anara-ka and they camped within a niche that protected them from the hostile cold winds that bite like the giant wolves. The next day, they found ruins of an ancient tower in the valley behind Anara-ka, but Freya would not speak of them other than to say it was of the first civilization that lived in the world and that the less known about them, the better. The winds had grown stronger and kept the two from traveling any further than to the valley behind the next mountain, Zatorin-ka. After three days and two more battles with wolves that left Styrkar with a mangled left leg and after which he outright refused to turn back, they reached the base of Hathan-ka.

Despite his injuries, he took to scaling the mountain while Freya waited in a cave in the valley with the horses and wolves. With the orb, the resin he had found on the dead adventurer and provisions to last him for several days, if he was careful, Styrkar ascended the steep face of Hathan-ka. Even on the lower levels, the wind threatened to tear him from the rocks and throw him into the valleys of the other mountains or even into the other mountains themselves. But he was undaunted in his quest as he clawed his way up the black rocks toward the summit.

It took him several days, during which he rested and ate little. When he did rest on Hathan-ka's narrow cliffs, he would look down from his lofty heights and into blackness where valleys should be. As he neared the summit, he could hear the howling and hissing from the Other Gods. Despite their warnings, Styrkar pressed on.

Finally, he reached the top of Hathan-ka, where the wind whistled and howled deafeningly. His long fingers were raw and bleeding and he shivered uncontrollably. In the twilight sky, he could spot the shadowy forms of the Other Gods drawing near to him as he took out resin from the Tree of Life and set fire to it with flint and steel. Then he sat on his knees and mediated and prayed to his gods when suddenly, they spoke to him in his mind. They knew he was Styrkar, whose mother was Astrid of the City of Ice and that they had been waiting for him. Before him they placed two seeds, one a dull green and the other a dull golden brown and they told he had to go to the place men called the Spectre Wood, to the stumps of the old trees, and place the seeds in them. Then, he was to break the orb of the old trees' essence and pour it over the seeds. This, they emphasized in voices that were neither man nor woman, had to be done as fast as Styrkar could ride there. Once completed, the trees would grow anew and the Son of Arnkell could resume his revenge upon Aethelwulf and Baat'zaar. At no time, did the gods, either the Old Ones or the Other Ones, ever reveal their true forms, remaining at best only shades against the jagged rocks and perpetually dark skies.

After resting, Styrkar took the large seeds into his belt pouch and began a slow and painful descent to Hathan-ka's base where Freya awaited him. She did not ask the young warrior what the gods had asked of him, nor did he tell, as they headed back to the ice city. There he remained for four days as Freya and Wograven tended to his bloodied fingers, his throbbing, twisted leg and the hypothermia from his climb. They also cared for his animals. When he decided he had to go, they begged him to stay longer, for they knew he was not well, but Styrkar told them he had no choice but to do the gods' quest and to destroy Baat'zaar and Aethelwulf once and for all. He left with them as a token of his gratitude the horses of Prince Harwulf and Prince Bardo.

So from the frigid northern lands of perpetual twilight, Styrkar rode south and headed for the Spectre Wood, where he would put the seeds of the Two Trees into the dead stumps and water them with the essence of the former Trees.

A month had passed since Styrkar had vanished into the north and many considered him dead. Rumors abounded that he had met his end at the hands of Aethelwulf, who sought his death as revenge for the deaths of his sons, while others say he died trying to reach the frozen wastes of the Forbidden Lands, killed by the fiendish creatures that dwelled there. In any case, he entered into the Nordlands and headed for the Spectre Wood without incident.

Aethelwulf, thinking his foe had died, ceased his search and focused his attention on Aardsberg. Unlike Murtha and the smaller cities, Aardsberg was better defended and could not have been taken as easily with the size of the units Aethelwulf had sent out in searching for Styrkar. One had tried and was quickly annihilated by the Blue Tyger knights. And while the king knew that the Horsemen had made their home in Tuska, he could not reach it easily without first taking a border city to establish a supply line, a

matter he had not thought of addressing with Vegard before he razed Murtha.

His folly also had another unexpected effect, one he did not notice until his forces had

regrouped-the number of his men had suffered. Attacks by Horsemen and failed attempts

to mete out destruction upon the larger of the border cities had greatly decimated his

forces, so Aethelwulf would have to hire -something he was extremely reluctant and too

impatient to do. He decided to first try to take Aardsberg with what men he had.

Without having Vegard, Harwulf or Bardo to lead his forces, it seemed he had to it

himself, but he brought Kaisa with him, for the invasion on Aardsberg was the main

reason he had kept her alive and under his control. Convinced Styrkar was dead and that

she had no hope of surviving the battle on Aardsberg, she grudgingly helped him with his

plans, although she believed she had arranged it so the dread king would meet his demise,

as would she. She had placed him into a position she figured inescapable for his troops

and would allow her to kill him while the forces of Aardsberg killed them.

What Kaisa did not count on was Aethelwulf turning the command of the invasion over

to his brother-in-law Ketil. The king would observe from a safe distance with his elite

guard, for although Kaisa was under his control, someone told him to not trust her. One

of the adepts among Darfos's clerics betrayed his oath of secrecy and let it be known to

Aethelwulf that she was to betray him at a critically important moment and to assassinate

him or arrange his death.

Ketil was not an intelligent or wise man and it was no secret that the king had hated him.

With his wife and children all dead, Aethelwulf felt nothing holding him back from

killing this feebleminded man. So Kaisa and Ketil led the Stromgald forces into battle, much to the her horror, and to their deaths, for they were all trapped and Aardsberg's forces, as well as the Horsemen who had rode up from Tuska to help with the defenses, fell upon them mercilessly. Kaisa fought against Stromgald as well, but the spells cast upon her activated and her life was taken from her before she could get too many of the invaders.

Thorbjorn had seen her and initially thought of his dream some time ago of riding up on a blackguard in battle, but when she fell, screaming in agony from the spells, he knew she had not truly fallen from grace. He took her body back to Tuska, where she was buried as a champion of Aardsberg and Tuska.

The bodies of the men of Stromgald were not so favorably treated. Ketil was not killed, but he was made to hang over the marble gates of Aardsberg for days as he starved to death. They refused to take his body down even as birds fed from the remains, for they wanted to send home the loss to Aethelwulf. The men of Stromgald who did not die in battle were put in put into wicker and set on fire in the golden city's main square, screaming as they burned.

Aethelwulf witnessed from a distance the failed invasion and was not surprised. He had expected it to be a mass human sacrifice and it was. He smiled at having rid himself of Ketil and for the invasion going as expected, but he was not happy. He rode back with his remaining forces to his palace in Stromgald, thinking all the while of his four children, heirs to the throne, who were now all dead within months. He also had to talk to Baat'zaar.

Once in the safety of his fortress, Aethelwulf went into the secret rooms hidden behind his own bed chambers. None in the Nordlands had knew of his powers as a sorcerer and it was a secret he had been able to keep very well, thanks to hidden library where he kept his books on spells and talismans and the rooms where he had his altars to gods better left unspoken and his teleportation circles. He went into his lab there and took some leaves and incense and a copper colored powder and put them in a brazier in the room with the teleportation circle. He lit them using a cantrip and then with his booming voice chanted the incantation that caused the runes on his floor to glow a vile, blood red and a great vortex of copper and red light swirled in the air before him, with its lowest point on the floor. Aethelwulf stepped through the vortex and into the strange, minaret city of Baat'zaar. There, he sought out the demon lord and they discussed sending an army of demons to aid him, for none except Aethelwulf and Baat'zaar knew that, prior to sending the Stromgald troops to their death, the king had pledged their souls, including Kaisa's, to the Abyss. With the price paid, the fiend agreed to give him an army of ten thousand demons led by another demon lord who ranked just below Baat'zaar, Nephraim, to take over the lands where the most vital portals in the hub existed.

Nephraim was not as civilized as Baat'zaar, but when Aethelwulf laid eyes upon him, he knew he had the power to take Aardsberg and Tuska and the other realms of the world. The subordinate demon lord was a brute of a creature, looking like a minotaur, but with four long, black horns and red glowing eyes sitting upon a torso that bore two overlong muscular arms that ended in massive fists. His lower body was that of a dragon's tail and he spoke in grunts through teeth that jutted out at odd angles from his mouth. The very air around this demon was foul and malevolent and Aethelwulf was pleased with his new commander.

And then Baat'zaar gave him a champion-Kaisa, for now her soul had been sent into the Abyss and had become corrupted by its fate. She was brought before him and looked as she did in life, but had that unwholesome, evil slant to her eyes and wore the blood red armor of the Knights of Darfos and Aethelwulf was pleased with his new champion. Before sending Aethelwulf back, Baat'zaar promised to send his white ships, too, when the time came and allow the king to use them to sail to other lands to capture the portals there as well. Aethelwulf thanked him deeply and returned to his chambers a very happy man.

Styrkar reached the Spectre Wood without much incident and camped just inside its boundaries among the healthy, newer trees. He again looked over his map, which he had purchased from a traveling merchant and had modified as far as places within the forest itself; marking the location of the ruins he had seen prior-the ones he had been in with Kaisa and Thorbjorn and the very ancient ones he had descended into on his way to the Forbidden Lands. Using the journal, he could make out the location of the Marshes of the Dead. There were areas he had hoped to avoid, such as the place where no creature or spirit would go, but realized that he may have to pass by them without actual knowledge of their location. He had found maps drawn crudely in the back of the journal, but he could not be certain on their accuracy after reading about how one becomes disoriented in areas of the forest so that all direction was the same.

His mind wandered to thoughts of Kaisa for some reason when he thought of that place no spirit would go, He had not seen her since he had been captured by Baat'zaar and he wondered where she was now and if she was still alive, for surely by now, things here must have changed. And then he remembered Wograven never told him what those pages from the room far below the Spectre Wood had said.

It mattered little now to him anyway as he headed once again into the haunted forest, to those unholy places. As he entered the place where the trees were ancient and wicked, he noticed a gypsy wagon and was stopped in his path by Desdinova, who greeted him by name. This time, she spoke to him of his quest and offered help in exchange for one of his horses. Styrkar asked her which she wanted and she pointed to his own warhorse, for it was stronger and smaller and she was partial to the horses of Fantoft. He gave her his warhorse and put all of his things on his the one he took from the sergeant. She then told him, as she tied his horse to the front of her wagon, that he probably knew that the place in the ancient city where the great stumps moldered away was that place where he had to go to plant the Tree seeds the gods gave him. She said the city had been that of his mother's people before the ices receded and the great battles took place. She even offered to guide him to those Tree stumps, so that he might avoid the unholy places in the journal. When he asked her how she knew of the journal, she first smiled and spoke to him of his tripping over words and how odd it was a great warrior and child of so brave a father and so powerful a mother would have such an affected voice. Then Desdinova explained that she knew everything, especially that which is in her forest. For Lady Desdinova was not just a gypsy, but was the dryad who dwelled within the Tree of Life. It still lived, for it still produced resin, and it would only truly die when the new tree was planted, in which she would dwell in and tend to for all eternity. Her sister had dwelled within the Tree of Wisdom, but had died when that Great Tree was destroyed after the battles that cursed the very earth and forest with the evil committed in it.

She asked Styrkar what he knew of those battles and smiled broadly at his ignorance of the subject. Desdinova spoke of the Trees existing long before even the first civilization and that that was when she was born. The papers he had found and that Wograven never explained to him were from that civilization, but she said nothing more about what was on them. She did say that it was better left unknown what the beings that lived at that time were like and what they had done, but she would tell him the one thing they did that was not demonic-when they discovered the Trees, they built a holy city around them. When their civilization had died, the second, which the tomb that he had found with Thorbjorn and Kaisa on their first journey here, belonged to, built their holy city over the ruins of the first. This continued for the next three civilizations until the People of the Ice fled to the Forbidden Lands where the sun never rises. No matter how good or evil the civilization had been, they were always wise enough to guard and care for the trees.

And not all of the Ice People left immediately. The druids, who his mother's family belonged to, remained to tend to the trees despite the increasing temperatures. Desdinova and her sister Diamanda, dryad of the Tree of Wisdom, foresaw the horror that was to come and gave them the Trees' essences. The Trees had produced one seed each and those seeds, which Styrkar possessed now, had been given to the druids long before the visions of doom and in turn, they gave them as offerings to the Old Ones.

With the horse hitched to the wagon, she and Styrkar rode side by side as they continued their talk. Desdinova asked him what he knew of what had happened here and was amused to hear that all he knew was a battle occurred where some sort of evil or terrible atrocities had cursed the land. She explained that the battle was part of a war that had flowed out of the Abyss, a power play between demons and devils that started with a certain fiend named Darfos and his minion Baat'zaar. Darfos had been the general of a god whose name was better left unmentioned and sought to usurp that god's place in the ancient pantheon. With Baat'zaar's help, he gained a cult of dedicated followers and the service of some powerful devils and they tried to outright overthrow the god, but the god proved too powerful and a war that would last a thousand years broke out.

The world that Desdinova and Styrkar lived in was somehow a hub for travel to other planes-they all converged in various locations of this planet. It was believed the oldest civilization had established these portals, but not much exists of their writings except for translations by an obscure wizard said to have existed in the days of the fourth civilization, but who was never a part of the civilization itself known only as Eroc the Lost. All that was known about him was that he was able to translate things none before nor since have been able to decipher and that what ancient knowledge he held allowed him to know things that no mortal should have known. In Eroc's tomes, he described the portals, how to activate them and their locations on the planet, one of which happened to exist near the Trees, where in the journal it described a certain stone circle.

It was because of these portals that the world was valuable and desired by the devils, for it would allow them to travel to the planes and acquire power or destroy other entities at will. Capture of this world eluded Darfos and after centuries of battling other gods and devils for it, he fell complacent in his efforts to gain it. Baat'zaar must have gotten power hungry for those portals and tired of serving what he viewed as a weak master and decided that he would try for the world himself, only Baat'zaar decided to handle things differently. First, he had established his presence among men by using his demons as merchants. Then, he used men to carry out his conquests-men such as Aethelwulf, who were evil in their hearts and felt no loyalty to their own kind.

Mortals had gotten involved in the thousand year war as well. The clerics of the other pantheons fought the priests of Darfos in the forest where the portal stood. Some of the souls were killed and lay sleeping eternally in the swamps on that side where the Spectre Wood approached the Sea of Mystics. The adventurer in the journal was wise to not reach in and touch the cadaver, for the bizarre qualities of the water has preserved them all these centuries. And it is not just mortal men who lay in that natural mass grave, but demons and devils as well, although they cannot be seen unless you go into the more dangerous reaches of the swamp.

She mentioned a place near the swamp and off the shore. It was a city that had been inundated during the battle and that on a day when the sun or moon was clear in the sky, you could see the ruins far below in the dark waters. Desdinova said it was not a mortal city, but hinted that they had not been ruins either of the old civilizations, and that they were part of the cursed battlefield, but she did not say what had happened there. He asked her if she had visited the place at all. She shook her head, and then said she viewed it when it was not submerged from afar.

At this point, Desdinova could see through the trees one of the great stones of the portal ring and guided her wagon away from it. She warned Styrkar to not go to it until he should ever learn how to activate the portal safely. As they rode away, Styrkar could have sworn he had seen one of the pillars move on its own volition, but he was not sure if he was merely hallucinating that it had moved. He did not say anything of it to Desdinova.

Of the area where nothing grew, she never brought it up, nor did she mention the cemetery, but she told him of the ghosts and shades. She told him they were damned souls who took part in the war between Darfos and his god that were forever bound to the forest to repeat their part in the battle, every sadistic act of it every night. During the day, they would go to the Abyss where their souls were tortured in unimaginable ways. They spoke to mortals who passed through the forest in hopes that one might find a way to release them from their torment. Then she told him she doubted that anything could be done, although Styrkar cared little about their problems.

Desdinova also told Styrkar about Kaisa. The lady paladin had quit her order upon hearing he had fallen overboard of one of Baat'zaar's ships and was presumed drowned. She then took Arnkell's sword and his horse and weapons to fulfill revenge upon Aethelwulf in his name, but wound up doing an incredibly stupid thing-joining the dreadful king's army in hopes of assassinating him. She was bound by spells to Aethelwulf, but still sought to betray him and was killed by the enchantments Darfos's clerics and wizards had placed upon her. Aethelwulf, prior to the battle in which she died, had pledged her soul to Baat'zaar in the Abyss and Desdinova could only fear what it meant. Styrkar felt his heart sink upon hearing the news and vowed he would rescue her soul and send her to Valhalla so he could join her in death when the time. Desdinova laughed and muttered a word he never had heard before. Seeing his raised eyebrow and blank stare, she told him she called him a "Nephilim" and went on to explain that was what the People of the Ice were-mortals who bred with angels, or in the case of the People of the Ice, with another planar creature, although what that creature had been was lost to time.

That night, he rested in the wagon with her and played with his large, black whelps. Desdinova thought they were oddly big for wolves and asked him where he had found them. He said he had taken them from the Hazor Peaks after defending himself against the wolves there. She regarded him with wide eyes and nodded her head, for no man had ever successfully been to the Hazor Peaks, let alone had seen the gods or return with the dreaded wolves for his war dogs.

His dreams that night were of Kaisa and they were pleasant ones-memories of when they were in the deserts of the Abyss and when she first took him in after he had been ridiculed for being a beggar. She never had made fun of when he stumbled over his words; in fact, he keenly believed she loved it. He knew that even if her soul were corrupted, she could not be happy in the Abyss serving the devils there and in his dreams, he saw himself riding into Baat'zaar's city on a great grey warhorse and with the two great Wolves of Hazor tearing demons trying to stop him and taking her for the final time into his arms. He would ride her to Valhalla himself and force the guardians there to let her in even if it meant he himself would forever be damned.

The next afternoon, Styrkar had arrived at the ruins of the People of the Ice and his eyes beheld the two trunks, their size rivaling that of lakes and palaces, but black and smelling of decaying wood. One had the green and brown resin upon its phosphorescent fungi covered bark and Desdinova allowed him to remove some of the crystals from the dying tree. Then he climbed upon the rotting stump of what was once the great Tree of Life and stepped gingerly across the soggy surface to the center, which was more soil-like than wood-like and he took the giant pine seed and buried it deep into the stump. He did the same with the acorn of the Tree of Wisdom. He took the flask of his parents' ashes and used the base to carefully break open the orb and he poured the essence of the trees into the flask, an act that surprised even the wise Desdinova. He gently mixed it by rotating the metal flask and pouring half onto each place he buried the seeds. The dryad did not understand why he had used his parents' flask and guessed by the vague look upon his face that maybe he did not fully understand that action or was not sure if whatever reason he did it was going to work. She never asked him and he never told his reasons.

As he walked back to her, shrugging his shoulders in confusion, she could feel the power left in the stump wax as the orb's contents and the ashes of one of the Children of Ice were poured upon it and the rush of that power as it left the dying tree and fed the new tree. Styrkar could not sense it and apologized for nothing happening, but she told him he had indeed succeeded and she thanked him for reviving the Trees. In time, the energy would spread throughout the Spectre Wood and he would be surprised on the transformation should he ever return.

The destruction of the orb was not felt only by Desdinova. The ripples of the breaking and emptying of the primordial glass were felt all the way to the Abyss and Baat'zaar, who sought the power of the Great Trees' essence to conquer the nations where the portals existed and to defeat Darfos, screamed as if his soul were wrenched from him. He cursed Styrkar's name for destroying the orb and he knew the Son of Arnkell would inevitably hunt him down for his part in the deaths of his parents and of Kaisa.

With the Gods' quest finished, Styrkar rode out of the Spectre Wood alone and spurred the palomino mount for Aardsberg, where he would devise a plan on liberating Kaisa's soul from the Abyss. He would not have to fret over the problem for too long, for he was barely a stone's throw from the Spectre Wood when he encountered a column of

Baat'zaar's demon warriors with Kaisa and Nephraim leading them to Aardsberg as well.

She looked different than he remembered her. Gone were her compassionate eyes, now

replaced with ones that were cold and reptilian. She carried herself arrogantly and she

had no sign of the humility or humbleness she had had in life. Styrkar rode to confront

her anyway, hoping that at least something in her would recall who he was. As he

approached, the demons began to call for his death. He did not come too close, for he

knew that the fiends would sadistically kill him now that he no longer possessed the orb

of the Trees' Essence.

Upon seeing Styrkar riding more than a few yards away, Kaisa spurred her horse and

rode to him. She regarded him at first as an inferior foe, glaring haughtily from her dark

devil horse. He returned her contemptuous look and asked her for his father's sword, for

she had taken it to do what she had thought he could no longer do and she failed at it. Her

malevolent eyes stirred in thought and softened considerably. The memory hit her

distorted, twisted mind that she had fled her order to kill Aethelwulf for Styrkar, who she

had believed to be dead. She could not remember why she did not carry out her self-

imposed mission or where Arnkell's sword was now.

Seeing in her emerald eyes and in the vague expression on her face that she could not

remember the last days of her life, Styrkar grabbed the reins of her dreaded horse and

drove his horse back into the Spectre Wood. Of the many demon warriors, only those

who sought favor from Baat'zaar and not Darfos attempted to chase down the two before

they reached the forest, but failed to do so. Styrkar had Kaisa alone in the sanctuary of

the Great Trees and the ancient hallowed city of no less than five ancient civilizations.

Kaisa demanded him to tell her what he had done that caused Baat'zaar to despair and anger so at the same time and he confessed to destroying the orb that had been the obsessions of the demon and Aethelwulf. She blinked her eyes, startled by this, for she had known Styrkar had been entrusted to protect it. He further explained that its destruction was the point of his whole quest-it had to be destroyed to accomplish something else more important.

He knew why she had gone to Stromgald and why she had joined Aethelwulf's army. He also knew that she must be unhappy, for she had been in life a great and loyal knight, and he had taken her from the demons in an effort to rescue her soul from the Abyss. She at first scoffed him for doing what he had done, but revealed she was indeed unhappy in the Abyss and that she did not want to spend eternity serving on a demon lord's agenda. At that, he uttered a prayer to his gods to send the soul of his foe to them as he drew his long sword and battle axe and attacked her outright. Her eyes widened in surprise and she barely got her sword out to deflect his blows. She pleaded with him, but he continued his attacks, saying only that he had to fight her and barely giving her any chance to attack him herself. Using his battleaxe, he caught hold of her leg and flung her violently to the ground before stepping forward and cleaving down upon her skull with his sword. She spasmed violently, dropping her sword, as the soul left the body in which it was imprisoned and went spiraling into the afterlife, leaving Styrkar alone and wondering whether what he did was successful. He did not regret it, though, as he rode through the haunted wood toward Stromgald to get his father's sword back and to finish the vengeance he had started.

The mighty king was not in his castle when Styrkar came to call. He had left to join his

demon army, leaving behind a meager watch. Again, the Nordman remembered his father

telling him about the escape tunnels in castles so the royal family could flee from

imminent doom and he skulked about at night to find it. Find it he did, a small cave

entrance under a small, cold waterfall. He crept along the tunnel and emerged in a

passageway between walls in the palace itself. The door was a secret panel in

Aethelwulf's library, in which was two stories of fancily carved shelves holding tomes

collected by the once noble kings of Stromgald for hundreds of years.

One book sat with its pages open upon a lectern in the center of the room and Styrkar's

curiosity got the better of him. He examined the pages and found the book to be one of

the obscure scribe Eroc's works describing the planar portals of the world. It described

where each of these portals led and how to activate each one. The pages were open to a

section describing a portal that could be used to transport to any of the countless levels of

the Abyss, depending upon the sacrifice given at its portal's altar. Of the portals in the

book that were described, this was the only one Eroc had not given its location. Styrkar

examined the book and found notes in the margins, apparently added by Aethelwulf or

one of his scribes. The locations in the days of the author were called by different names

than what the world knew them as at this time and some of the marginal notes were

attempts at pointing out what the current names were. None were on the pages of the

Abyss portal. Styrkar suspected that was the feared portal in the Spectre Wood, although

a note on another page betrayed Aethelwulf's knowledge of this portal and that he

designated it as a door to the Shadow Plane and that it was no longer working.

Upon comparing both sections, it dawned upon Styrkar that perhaps Aethelwulf's dismissal of the Spectre Wood portal was wrong, for the description of the place of the Shadow Plane portal did not match up to anything that would have been in that area even in those early days. It did, however, describe in gory detail the necessary actions needed to travel to any place in the Abyss, including a level that had a great harbor that connected to a vortex in the middle of the Great Ocean and was a vast desert with a city of delicate minarets, a place Styrkar recognized immediately.

The library was attached to the royal bedroom, where a painting of the deceased queen hung over a lavish, canopy bed made with satin sheets. The furniture was all of ebony imported from lands Styrkar knew nothing or little of and bore gilded carvings of the crests of Stromgald and Fantoft and Skjold and of the old royal families that ended when Aethelwulf usurped the throne. A great stone fire place carved and depicting a moment in the Nordland's fabled past stood dark and quiet across the bed. It was not centered, though, sitting closer the wall on its left, and this bothered him. He walked to that wall and noticed that the gilding looked newer and shinier than that upon the other walls. Along that wall were the busts of the heroic kings of Stromgald, all crafted from alabaster and Aethelwulf saw fit to add Vegard and Bardo's busts, also in alabaster, to the far end with and inscription on their heroism as princes of the realm.

Then Styrkar noticed a rather curious addition among the kings-King Vidar. Vidar was not a prominent king-he accomplished nothing great in his reign and by those Nordlanders of Stromgald and Skjold who sailed the seas, he was referred to as the "King of Doldrums" for the lack of anything, good or bad, happening. The head of the bust sat unevenly upon the shoulders. He grabbed the sculpture by its beard and lifted it up to reveal a lever. The lever, when pulled and not pushed or turned, opened a door between the Doldrums King and another royal head.

The door led to a chamber full of burns and with a circle of symbols carved into stone floor and a door on the far end. It was Aethelwulf's casting room where he apparently tested his summoning spells.

A servant had entered the king's chambers while Styrkar was in the room and noticed the casting room's secret door wide open. Curiously, she went to this room and came face to face with Styrkar. He drew his sword as she screamed and killed her without a word and left her body there, taking care to close the door behind him.

A guard ran into the room as he poured himself a drinking horn of the king's wine. When the man demanded who he was, he answered that it was of no concern to anyone and when he ordered him to tell him what happened here, despite Styrkar standing there with a bloody sword in his left hand, the Son of Arnkell asked him where the king's arms were kept. The guard threatened him with death and Styrkar told him that if he said it, he must do it. The guard drew his sword and let out a battle cry as he lunged at the towering Nordman, who casually raised his dripping weapon and killed him. He calmly left the room afterward, still holding the drinking horn of wine in his right hand and his sword in his left, swinging it about like a cane and flinging droplets of blood on the fine rugs and walls.

He roamed the halls going from room to room, killing any who discovered his presence and refilling his drinking horn once, until he found the king's armory. Styrkar found it locked and sighed as he drew his battleaxe to hack on the masterly carved and crafted door. His bashing caught the attention of a guard looking for a killer loose within the palace and he came face to face with Styrkar. When the man demanded who he was, he answered that it was of no concern to anyone and when he ordered him to tell him what happened here, despite Styrkar standing there with a battleaxe in his left hand, the Son of Arnkell asked him where the key to the king's armory was kept. The guard threatened him with death and Styrkar told him that if he said it, he must do it. The guard drew his sword and let out a battle cry as he lunged at the towering Nordman, who casually hacked down his axe and killed him. Once he killed the guard, he resumed hacking upon the door until it splintered from one particularly strong blow.

Within were all of the swords and weapons and armor of the old kings and princes as well as those weapons he stole from the bodies of the Horsemen he had his minions murder. He found on a rack his father's sword and the alien blade of the dog men. In a chest were the battleaxe and the long sword and the armor he had won in the Challenges of the Pyramids in the Abyss. Then he found the sword of Kaisa before she became a blackguard, when he knew her in life. More guards, this time three, ran up on him as he strolled out carrying the weapons he came for and his proper armor he so rightfully won. When they demanded who he was, he answered that it was of no concern to anyone and when they ordered him to tell them why he was here, despite Styrkar standing there with a battleaxe in his left hand and armed to the teeth, the Son of Arnkell asked them where was the king's bath. The guards threatened him with death and Styrkar told them that if they said it, they must do it. The guards let out a battle cry as they lunged at the towering Nordman, who casually quickly dispatched each with angry cleaves to their heads, sending blood and cerebral matter splashing on the walls and ceilings.

He found the king's bath and this time, when a young, blonde maid walked in on him, he ordered her to fetch him some bath water, soap, linens and the best wine and mead the king owned. When she demanded who he was, he answered that he was Styrkar, Son of Arnkell and snarled at her to not question his orders or he would kill her where she stood. The maid fetched the things he required and when he ordered her to clean his things, she did so without question. He ordered her to fetch him one of the king's Nordlander tunics and she found a black and red one for him and helped him dress and put on his armor from the Challenges. Finally, he ordered her to the pantry to get meat for his whelps and he told her where to take the food. If his dogs wound up dead from foul or questionable means, he vowed in his deepest voice that he would find her within the castle and disembowel her. He added that she must stock his horse with several bottles of the finest wine from the wine cellar.

After finding the trail of dead bodies left in Styrkar's wake and the word from the maid who the intruder was, the rest of the castle staff ran the opposite way when they saw him coming through the halls, even the guards, for this was the man who killed Bardo and Vegard and who Aethelwulf himself destroyed the family and tribe of. As Styrkar had come to the palace, so he left, through the secret passage, although the staff thought his disappearance was of a divine nature. He rode off in search of Aethelwulf and Baat'zaar and those remaining invaders of his village.

One such as Styrkar does not escape the notice of the higher devils and Darfos found him most annoying, yet most impressive. He appeared before the Son of Arnkell on his way to find Aethelwulf as a hooded man of swarthy skin and with one patch over his eye. Darfos made no deception about who he was and that he appeared in a mortal's form to make it easier for the two of them to talk. He knew Styrkar sought revenge against Baat'zaar for his part in the whole affair and admitted that he himself sought the mutinous fiend's death. Since both sought the same end with different motives that perhaps a deal could be reached between them. The offer was for Styrkar to be Darfos's champion against the demon lord in return for the arch devil's aid in his quest of revenge against King Aethelwulf and the ones who killed his parents and destroyed his village. He know who the remaining men were and where they were at and all that Styrkar needed to do to get that information was to agree to the bargain. He further assured Styrkar that his soul was not going to be forced into the Abyss for all eternity, a condition of most such bargains, for he could not lay claim to the souls of those touched by other planes, just as Baat'zaar could not despite any threats he made, and, even if he could, he would soon find himself in the same position with the Nordman as he was with Baat'zaar, an out of control minion bent on usurping from him his position that he so rightfully stole.

Styrkar agreed, for he doubted his ability to deal with a warlock king and a demon alone, but insisted that the contract only be by word, for any mark would, he feared, bound him to servitude in the Abyss. At that, Darfos teleported him to the city in the Abyss to kill the demon lord there, for no other place could a demon or devil be destroyed except in their home plane.

Styrkar looked at the empty drinking horn he had pilfered from Aethelwulf and filled it with wine he stole from the same king as he walked with the whelps to Baat'zaar's palace, a large bronze, copper and brass domed hall in the center of the city. The demon lord awaited him, a bronze weapon in each hand and in the reddish bronze fiend-forged armor of his status. He regarded the mortal foe with burning eyes and hissed his displeasure at seeing him, expressing especially his anger at Styrkar's destruction of the orb and releasing Kaisa's soul from the Abyss. The Nordman dumped what was left of his wine on the ground as his adversary complained of his interference and tucked the drinking horn into his belt. He ordered the wolves of Hazor to sit and stay as he drew his battleaxe and long sword and the two flung themselves at each other.

Weapons clanged and crashed as the two fought furiously to kill each other. As their battle raged on, other fiends in the city stopped what they were doing or came out to watch, with no sound and no emotions. Styrkar hacked off one of Baat'zaar's limbs, and then another and both times the demon howled in pain and slashed at him more ferociously. The blood that spilled from his stumps coagulated and steamed and from it rose mephits that attacked Styrkar, but the Horseman remained focused on Baat'zaar, knowing that if he went for the smaller, lesser fiends, he would be sliced to pieces. The melee ranged slowly from the main doors of the palace, through the city's plaza and into the marketplace, lasting for several hours and leaving blood drizzled and splattered from one end of their battlefield to the other. Another limb flew off and more mephits attacked Styrkar and he began feeling himself fading and his vision darkened as his injuries grew extensive and festered. One of Baat'zaar's blows to Styrkar's armor, though, set off something neither expected, for the armor was made of the hides of hellhounds and it imbued with an enchantment that caused it to flare up randomly when struck. The demon, while not hurt by it, was startled and the Nordman took advantage of the pause. He mustered up the last of his energy and cleaved blindly at Baat'zaar, his axe sinking deep into something soft and the beast howled as if all the Abyss were being destroyed in holy fire and it deafened Styrkar's ears, So powerful, too, was cleave that it kept going into several mephits. There was a great din of bronze swords falling while he chopped in the air at mephits, hearing their cries as he killed them, before all that was left was a whistling breeze cutting through the silence.

He dropped to his knees near the body of Baat'zaar and several demons approached him cautiously. One of them asked him as he knelt there, bleeding from his head and chest and arms, if he needed any help. This struck Styrkar as odd, as demons and devils normally are not in the business of healing unless it involves them getting some favor or soul in return. He questioned the motives of these demons, which in response smiled and exclaimed the favor was already done in killing Baat'zaar, for these few sought to usurp the demon lord and had been unsuccessful. Reluctantly and against his better judgment, he allowed them to do so, so long as they did not take his soul or bind him to some nearly impossible quest. As they were healing him, though, Darfos gated the Nordman and his horse and wolves back to his own plane, where he healed him completely.

The arch devil thanked him for ridding him of the demon lord and gave him his reward- Baat'zaar's helmet, a great steel helmet with horns that came down from the sides to the front of the face, and the information he needed to finish his revenge upon those who had killed his family years before. He now had the names and descriptions of all he sought and that all were laying siege to Aardsberg and other important cities north of the Spectre Wood. To his surprise, several of the names had been killed off in the same battle where Kaisa had died, where Aethelwulf through battle sacrificed souls to get his demon armies. He rode off to Aardsberg take care of the first of the surviving invaders, leaving Aethelwulf for the last. Baldwin and the Order of the Blue Tygers were having difficulty

defending the city from the demon army and several areas of the city had fallen to
Aethelwulf's army and yet, the brave paladin refused to call for the Horsemen in Tuska,
lest he appear to have to rely upon knights errant and barbarians and rangers to rescue
him and his order from any enemy. If paladins could not defeat demons and devils in
battle, then what were they there for, he reckoned. The result of his arrogance and pride
was that he was now defending only the palace of Aardsberg and a square mile of the city
from a vast and overbearing army from the Abyss.

Styrkar arrived at Aardsberg, with most of the golden city in ruin and flame. Dead bodies
laid strewn about the streets and the fountains and pools were dark red with blood. Those
who survived were blocked outside of the defended areas and were at the mercy of the
demon warriors, who tortured and raped all they found. Screams and howls filled the air,
but the newcomer to this invasion did not have an interest in stopping the invasion or
aiding Baldwin, for it was the academy ran by the Blue Tygers that called him "Kaisa's
Folly" and laughed at him for being a mere beggar.

He came upon a small unit of men from Stromgald and he recognized several from the
invasion upon his village. None recognized him, though, as he rode up calmly to them
with his two whelps walking next to his horse and the welcomed him, wondering if he
were from one of the other units. They did not like the use of the demons and deeply
despised Aethelwulf for allowing that female paladin and several companies to perish in
this same city earlier as a sacrifice to get these horrific fiends. As much as Styrkar burned
with desire to kill him, he had an idea hit him suddenly.

He asked them to tell him more about the demon army as he took out a bottle of the
king's wine and handed it to them as a bribe. And tell him they did. He found out they

could not die by normal means, by regular weapons. But magical weapons and holy water and best of all, a certain ritual by a cleric, could easily kill them or at least send them back to the Abyss. Styrkar listened and pretended to drink with them, all the while waiting until they fell asleep or an opportunity opened up for him to kill them. Finally, after Styrkar produced two more bottles from his horse, one big fellow with a long black beard asked him where such a sweet, red wine from and Styrkar grinned as he boasted taking it from Aethelwulf's cellars. They laughed, thinking him joking, until he told them that he was Styrkar, Son of Arnkell. They stopped laughing.

They were not sure if they should believe him when he drew Arnkell's sword, which they knew Aethelwulf had taken from the lady paladin he had discovered hiding among his troops. He repeated again that he was Styrkar, the Son of Arnkell, the man they murdered and that he had come to kill them for that murder. The men attacked him with their crudely made weapons, but in their inebriated state could not counter his blows from the great sword. Their blood and innards were cast about the campsite and when finished, Styrkar impaled their bodies onto wood stakes with a note to announce his presence:

"The Son of Arnkell hath come to mete out retribution! I come for Aethelwulf for those who destroyed my family and for any who decide to make my business their business!"

He looked through their things for anything he could use, deciding to grab several quivers, before riding off to find the others.

Three of Baldwin's paladins were trying to find the location of several catapults and ballistae when they spotted Styrkar riding along, not realizing he was not here to help them or that he had just brutally killed a unit of Aethelwulf's human warriors. They ran up to him and pleaded with him for his help in finding and destroying the siege weapons. At first, he berated them for the name calling he had received when he was younger and less experienced and that now that he had proven to be a better warrior than they were that suddenly they needed him to save their asses from the demon armies. Again, they pleaded with him, acknowledging that Baldwin would be angry if he knew they were asking the blackguard Kaisa's friend and Nordlander Horseman to aid them in battle, for paladins should be able to handle armies from the Abyss without help. At that, Styrkar agreed to help them, for he disliked Baldwin.

The four of them found the first ballista and ambushed the soldiers manning the weapon. They hacked the thing apart and set it on fire. Styrkar hacked the heads off the ballista crew and he impaled them on wooden stakes and stuck them around the burning siege weapon. They crept up on a catapult and found it manned by several of the tall, vile dog people. The four descended upon the beasts, which fought back fervently but eventually were defeated. Again, they destroyed the siege weapon and set it on fire, but this time, they threw the bodies of the beasts into the fire. Styrkar took another strange weapon as a trophy from the dead dog men-a knife of dark metal that curved with a handle between the two blades.

As they were leaving to find the next one, five Stromgald men attempted an ambush, jumping out from behind the ruins of a stone house. Even Styrkar did not know that the two wolves of Hazor had followed him and, when Aethelwulf's soldiers fell upon him and the paladins, the black wolves blasted the men of Stromgald with deathly cold breath that froze them solid and allowed their master and his cohorts to slaughter them easily.

The four managed to take down seven more catapults and two ballistae and their crews of men and dog men, with Styrkar collecting weapons he found of interest, when they peered over a mound and spotted for the first time a demon siege machine and its crew.

They were the veiled men seen before from the ghoulish ships and lurking about Tuska
and Aardsberg and over their faces, they still wore veils and shrouds, but now they wore
the red and black armor of the armies of the Abyss over those robes. The wolves of Hazor
wasted no time unleashing their freezing breath upon them, turning four of the infernal
things to ice. The fifth cried out an oath to Baat'zaar when Styrkar laughed with the news
that Baat'zaar was dead. At first, the beast did not believe him until he got a better look at
the helmet the Nordman wore. He lowered his sword and fled from the siege weapon,
calling out in the language of the Abyss that the demon lord was dead. Slowly, as the
news spread from one siege weapon to another and one platoon to another, the demons,
no longer bound to Baat'zaar and his deals, turned on Aethelwulf's men and began
devouring them. Those that escaped barely did so.

Aethelwulf, attempting to retreat, found himself battling Nephraim and managed to bind
the pit lord within a flawless, black gem by using an obscure incantation before finally
escaping to Stromgald. The battle, however, left him in considerably bad health, for the
demon's bites and weapons had damning effects upon mortals.

Styrkar refused to allow the destruction of the demonic siege machine. He had need of it
for a deed he felt he must do in the dread Spectre Wood and he and two of the paladins
rode into what was left of Aardsberg to retrieve two draught horses to aid in its
transportation. The tide was in the midst of turning when he rode in and, instead of being
welcomed with open arms for his part in saving the great city, Baldwin came screaming
red-faced. He berated his paladins for seeking the help of a beggar and an unworthy
soldier and then he turned his fury on Styrkar and it was then that it was clear that the
commander of Blue Tygers had been in love with one of his subordinate lady paladins,

Kaisa. He accused and blamed Styrkar of stealing Kaisa and sending her along the path to her Fall. He drew his blade and threatened to kill Styrkar and had to be held back by the Lord Mayor, Aesir, himself. The Mayor in turn cursed at Baldwin for threatening the one man who came to the aid of Aardsberg, for Aesir had no idea that Baldwin defied his orders to send for the Horsemen and put pride before saving the city.

When it became evident that the demons had turned on the warriors of Stromgald, Aesir thanked Styrkar and declared him a hero of Aardsberg and granted his request of two draught horses to remove a certain siege weapon from the battlefield to fulfill a self-imposed quest. It was also declared that, once the dead had been buried and areas of the city were secured, there would be celebration in Styrkar's honor for having been key in the defeat of the enemy. This had become too much for Baldwin and he fled from Aardsberg.

Styrkar was given the horses-one white and one black-and he left for the Spectre Wood, promising he would return before the festivities began. He traveled through, braving the whispering souls of the damned and the dreaded fog with its spirits battling one another in horrific battle until he had come to the center of the forest where the portal to all of the layers of the Abyss awaited. As he neared it, he realized with horror that what he had seen when he was traveling with Desdinova was not a trick of his eye. The stones that lay upon the ground, as he rode ever closer, began to rise to their place in the circle. This continued as he unhooked the horses and set them free and worked into position the hellish siege weapon. As he inspected the cannon, a purple aura glowed from one stone to the next. He took the hellish iron balls he had found and put on the machine to carry to this circle and he loaded one. Styrkar lit the fuse and with an ear-shattering roar and whoosh of smoke, the missile blasted forth and it destroyed one of the great monoliths. The stone exploded with a flash of violet fire and an ungodly din that deafened Styrkar for several days afterward and threw him several yards into a tree. When he came to, he found the cannon destroyed, but so was the portal. He collected the several of the heavy, rune-covered shards of the pulverized monolith and hid them in the ruins near the Great Trees, which peered now from the soil as if to make sure it was safe to come out. Except one shard, which he took with him.

He afterward returned to Aardsberg where he told Aesir all that had happened from the time he and Kaisa left for Tuska over a year before to the destruction of the portal. Despite Styrkar's struggle to speak of his adventures and quests, several bards and scribes were called and were retold everything that Aesir now knew and the word spread quickly through the town of the Great Styrkar and how he saved the world from the demon lord Baat'zaar and his minion Aethelwulf. A feast was held in his honor and, as the news spread from village to village and from city to city, more were dedicated in his name as a savior of the new kingdoms.

For the next five years, peace ruled as Aethelwulf found himself in no position to handle any invasion on Stromgald, let alone he invaded anyone else. His armies were sufficiently weakened and with no heirs to the throne, he was in dire need to remarry and reproduce, for his health had deteriorated. He had been beaten now, for sure, but he secretly rebuilt his armies and made his plans to try to capture the new kingdoms as he did the Nordlands, even if his original reason and his original supporters were no longer there. He wanted only one thing now, to destroy Styrkar, for had that infernal brat not ever survived and became a warrior, the entire continent would be his. Aethelwulf called the surviving soldiers of that raid where Arnkell had perished and he put them to the sword for failing to make certain that all in that village had indeed died, which was the only revenge he could mete out right now for the failed invasions and the loss of his children.

The new kingdoms of the Sea of Mystics spent their time rebuilding. Thorbjorn and the Horsemen rode to the ruins of Murtha and built upon it a new city, which was named Styrkarskog, after Styrkar. It was built around the fort the Horsemen had started constructing during Aethelwulf's invasions and Thorbjorn was made king.

Styrkarskog and Aardsberg both asked for Styrkar to come live within their walls, for he had taken part in leading the Horsemen and in saving the golden city, but he instead took up residence at Kjell's request in Tuska. Aesir there gave him quarters next to his livery stable, for he knew Styrkar was, before he was called upon by fate, a blacksmith. There, the softly-spoken, stuttering warrior could retire in anonymous peace. He was allowed to live there as long as he wanted, paying no taxes and no rent.

They were modest quarters, too-a large single room with the only other room being his kitchen, where a woman named Torill, a slave who had been a warrior from Stromgald and captured by Thorbjorn during the battle of Murtha, prepared his meals. He displayed his trophies on walls and shelves and a painting of Kaisa he had commissioned and oversaw personally and under where it hung upon his wall he had hung her sword. He kept the two wolves of Hazor there as well and they had litters of whelps, some of which he gave to Kjell and Thorbjorn and from which he gained the nickname The Hound Master. Despite his outward complacency and easy going nature, though, he still longed to kill Aethelwulf for the deaths of his parents, although now treaties with the dread king

for peace kept him from doing so.

In five years, the great cities had rebuilt and the world's memory faded. The tales of

Styrkar's feats had become folklore, as people added exploits to him or changed his name

in the songs altogether. It seemed Aethelwulf's invasions had been forgotten by all but

Aardsberg, Tuska and Styrkarskog.

Styrkar did not speak to the Stromgald slave for the better part of two years beyond

telling her what to fix for dinner or what sort of errands and chores she had to do. She had

been forbidden from consorting with the citizenry of Tuska, save for that which was

related to the tasks in which she had been ordered to do, such as buying food in the

market or materials to make tunics and rugs. The forced solitude was too much for her

one day while she was working on her loom there and she finally asked Styrkar who the

raven-haired, emerald-eyed woman was in the painting. She fully expected him to scold

her for talking to him and then beat her senseless, but without looking up from his

reading, he told her it was Kaisa, a lady paladin he knew once. She asked about Kaisa's

fate and he told her she was killed. When she offered sympathy, he glared at her and

informed her that it was her king who had been behind it, just as he had been behind the

deaths of the people in his village. Styrkar rose from where he had been reading and

strode up to her in a way that sent chills through her. He asked her in a deep voice her

name and she replied Torill. When he repeated it, it was as if he were repeating the name

of a hated devil, a tone she had only heard him reserve for the name of Aethelwulf. Torill

fully expected him to kill her with one of his weapons he kept in his flat, but he said nothing except that he sought the death of her king and he did nothing except head for his kitchen for some wine.

She went back to spinning wool and working on her loom before she thought of talking to him again, for she feared he would tell Lord Kjell she had spoken out of line. This time, though, Styrkar started the conversation. He asked her if she had ever been in Aethelwulf's castle. She answered that she had as a member of his personal guard before he began to rely upon binding demons and devils to serve him. Styrkar then asked her about how close she was to Aethelwulf and if she would still be able to get in and out of the castle with ease. Torill grew nervous with this line of questioning, for she knew he was planning to use it to kill the king she swore loyalty to. Yet, when she met Lord Kjell's secretary the next day in the market and told him of this, he told her to answer any question Styrkar asked or it would be recommended that she be put to death.

So Styrkar kept asking her questions, about Aethelwulf and the castle and anything else he felt was important and she reluctantly answered them as she would do her chores or weave her rugs on the loom. She learned from the detail and directness of some of his questions, although he never admitted it to her, that he had been in Aethelwulf's castle and that he was responsible for the deaths of at least two of the princes of Stromgald.

He had started going to his smithy regularly and one day, Torill was at the apartment when a shipment of bars of a strange bluish metal came, after which Styrkar had whisked them off. One day, he returned home carrying swords and axes made of oak and informed Torill, since she was a fighter in Stromgald, he was going to put her to good use by having her spar with him. Again, while she was out supposedly buying food for that night's dinner, she went to Kjell's secretary and told him of what Styrkar was having her do. She was told to do it, since she was formerly a fighter for the dread King Aethelwulf, or be put to death. So she was made to spar with him in the small courtyard outside his door and in the street in front of it.

Styrkar had been working on his new weapons-a long sword and a battleaxe-with which he planned to kill Aethelwulf. The metal was the rarest of all, having come to the world on a meteor, and he had managed to get some of the rare ore through Kjell and Thorbjorn's connections. After several weeks, he had made two weapons of his best work and he took those weapons to the Lord Mayor's war mage to place upon them enchantments to make them powerful enough to battle Aethelwulf and any of his servants. To do this, the wizard required of Styrkar the components to burn into the metal of the weapons to aid in the enchantments.

Upon returning to his apartment, he informed Torill she was to accompany him on some quests and he grinned in an evil way that sent chills into her spine. With Kjell's secretary watching his residence and his wolves, the Son of Arnkell rode off to collect five things needed for his swords, with his slave in tow on a mule. The five things were the heart of a dragon, the blood of the Dead God, the bones of one of the damned that lurked the Spectre Wood, a black opal and the musk of a Wolf of Hazor. The fifth component had already been delivered from one of his own wolves, which he had made Torill extract from the musk glands. They had to find the other four.

Styrkar decided to go to the Spectre Wood first, since he had grown quite familiar with it and those things that scared the normal men of the new kingdoms and the Nordlands no longer scared him, for he knew all of the secrets of the dreaded forest. Torill shook with fear and begged to be allowed to turn back when she realized Styrkar was going there first, for she had hoped he would seek out the dragon first and she could avoid going to the other places by being torn to shreds. He rode for the ruins where the two Great Trees had stood and whose seeds now grew again there to speak with Desdinova. The shadowy shapes fleeting through the trees and the voiceless whispers played at Torill's nerves and the fog rolling in from the swamp of the dead and the city under the sea sent shudders through her body, but Styrkar insisted upon continuing his ride to the ruins where Desdinova lurked. The warrior spirits again appeared, fighting and screaming and killing each other for a countless time. Then Styrkar heard something that he had not heard before and he froze his horse in its tracks to listen. It was a faint, far off sound of something slathering and hissing. His mind raced through stories his mother had told him…the gods…the creatures…the gods…the creatures…

He let out a half gasp and half shriek as his mind finally found what it was he had been told. Grabbing the reins of Torill's ass, he raced for any hiding place in hopes that what that noise belonged to would not sense their presence. The slave kept asking him what could possibly be so horrible to scare him if ghosts could not. Styrkar whispered for her to shut up as he found a ruin of a cottage and prayed to Tyr and Freya and Thor that it was enough to protect them. They scrambled into a corner and kept as quiet as possible, blindfolding the horses and holding them by their heads. The ungodly noise grew closer and closer and a smell like boiling pits of brimstone filled the air. It paused, then Styrkar heard it head off in another direction, apparently its attention attracted by something else it deemed more interesting or tasty. It felt like an hour that they waited instead of fifteen minutes before climbing on their mounts and heading for the ruins of the Ice People at full gallop through the thick, white fog.

Torill asked him again what they had been hiding from when she felt that they had

reached a fair distance for it to be safe to talk and Styrkar told her that his mother told

him that the gods that men worshipped and knew of were not the only gods and that there

were gods that should remain nameless. Those gods were the Other Ones. They were

older than the gods of men and even the many civilizations that have ruled the world. He

spoke, too, of Eroc the Lost, a sage unparalleled in his knowledge by any before or since,

save the forces of the supernatural, and his writings that these gods came from other stars

and other planes. He said both his mother and Eroc had described a god that fit what they

had heard and smelled and he cared not to utter its name, especially not with it lurking the

forest.

The spirits had returned to their home in the Abyss and the fog had started rolling out

when the two riders had reached the ruins where the two trees had stood and Styrkar

could see in the center of the Great Trees' stumps two new saplings, one with green

needles and one with gold leaves growing. A woman he barely recognized appeared, for

when he had last saw her, she had been older and a gypsy, but now she was youthful and

with long, cascading hair of forest green and glittering gold. Desdinova greeted Styrkar

warmly and again thanked him for planting the new trees, the pine tree having pulled the

energy from the old into its trunk and rejuvenating the dryad herself. She asked him what

had brought him to the forest and greeted the woman in slave rags that followed him.

Styrkar told her that Aethelwulf still lived and had signed a truce with the new kingdoms,

but he had a feeling that the peace with the dreaded king would not last long. Aethelwulf

would return and more powerful than ever. Furthermore, Styrkar wanted to create a

special set of weapons to finish his revenge. He wanted this parents' murderer killed by his own weapons crafted by his own hand that none have wielded besides him. To imbue them with the power, though, he needed a wizard and the wizard needed five things, the first was the musk of a wolf of Hazor, which was easy enough, although Torill cringed at the comment. The others he needed help with-the heart of a dragon, the blood of the Dead God, a black opal and bones of a damned soul in the Spectre Wood.

Desdinova told him that the bones could be found anywhere-all he needed to do was to go to those places where it looked like moss covered trees limbs and grab one protruding from the ground. He could also go to the swamp, although that was not highly recommended. She knew black opals existed but were rare and came from a specific river, although that river she did not recall the name of. She did know a sage who could probably tell them where that river was, however, and that he lived in the fabled Forest of Ever Night in the south. She had no idea where a dragon could be found, for none have been seen in ages and, even when they have, none knew where they lived. The Blood of the Dead God was the name of a gem found only in one series of caves in one of the ancient mountain ranges, but again, she did not know which one and suggested that he go to the sage. The sage was Olavi and he was very old, although she was not sure of how old. He said he knew Eroc and it was from Eroc he gained his knowledge, although unless he was one of the People of the Ice, that could not be possible in her eyes. He would do well to ride to Olavi in the Forest of Ever Night and speak with him. Styrkar thanked Desdinova and went to those parts of the woods that he and Kaisa and Thorbjorn had visited years before and grabbed one of the stone hard, moss-covered protrusions sticking out of the forest floor. He pulled up a large, petrified femur, which he stuffed into a saddlebag before riding through the Spectre Wood for the Forest of Ever Night.

The Forest of Ever Night was aptly named, for the canopy of the forest was even thicker than that of the Spectre Wood and one needed torches and candles to travel through it, even in the brightest of days. The trees, too, were tall with massive trunks and Styrkar felt many had been here since the days of the Great Trees. They were mostly gingko trees here, the oldest of all such trees, and great pines and it was here that the tall, dark-haired Children of the Forest dwelled. Like the Children of Ice, the people of his mother, they had old names they were called, but none called them those names anymore save Desdinova. They were "Nephilim", like Styrkar.

He and Torill came upon a village in the woods and asked where they could find Olavi the Sage. They directed him to an ancient gingko by the river where steps led high up into the canopy. They made the laborious climb up those stairs to a cottage in the crotch of the great main limbs where a light warmly glowed from a fireplace and candles within.

Styrkar entered and asked if he was Olavi. The man nodded and gestured for them to sit at his dusty, book laden table. He looked at Styrkar from under heavy white eyebrows and asked if he was the Styrkar of the legends. Amazed the man knew his name, the Son of Arnkell nodded as he took a seat in a black, knotty chair. Olavi gestured again to Torill, stating he did not differentiate between slave and warrior, and told her to have a seat. He asked Torill about her being captured in battle and why she had not been returned to her nation when the hostilities were over. She was amazed he knew she was a warrior and he confessed upon seeing her scars and noted that their locations were common to those who fought hand to hand battles. Torill explained her situation was because apparently Stromgald committed atrocities when they captured cities and any from Stromgald caught on the field were considered war criminals, subject to death. She had been captured and held in a dungeon in Tuska and was scheduled to be put to death by being drawn and quartered, but when Styrkar had arrived in the city to live, her sentence was commuted to life as a slave. Olavi asked her if Styrkar was a good master, a question Torill refused to answer. She admitted that any life was better than being in a dungeon and being put to death, though.

Olavi then spoke to Styrkar about his reason for coming. Styrkar told him of his desire to kill Aethelwulf, which was no secret to anybody in any part of the continent that had heard of the Son of Arnkell, and he told of the weapons he had created to do the job and what he needed for a wizard to imbue them with magic and that he had two-the musk of a wolf of Hazor and a bone of the damned from the Spectre Wood-but that he needed to know where to find the other three.

Olavi thought for a moment and then went to one of his many book shelves and looked over the titles before settling on one ancient tome with a peeling cover and binding. He flipped it open to a page and read from it about the Blood of the Dead God. The Blood of the Dead God referred to a gem indeed and it was located in a series of caves in the middle of the old mountains known as the Crystal Mountains. It was there that the god Abbath came to seek shelter to heal from his wounds from a battle with his brother Azatoth. He bled in his lair and that blood mixed with the minerals to create a crystal that was blood red with dark, foreboding eyes. They were said to have powers and were valuable to the seers and psions of the lands south of the Endless Wastes. It was also said that one of them was known to exist for certain outside of the cave, but had been buried in the tombs of Darksinger, the location of which was unknown.

The black opal was not what it seemed either-it was not a gem but a flower-a rare orchid that grew in the Shadow Wood and named for its black iridescence. Like the Forest of Ever Night, the Shadow Wood was an ancient forest of very tall trees that was outside of the ruins of the ancient city of Carvannia, where it was said that a likeness of Eroc stood with two of his three Bards in the plaza. The orchid grew high in the trees and would be no easy task to find and retrieve.

The final component, the dragon's heart, he said would be impossible-dragons, even the great Scythe Dragons, had not lived in the world, or at least have been spotted anywhere in the world, for decades, except by those who imbibed strange wines in excess. Olavi could not begin to tell them where such a creature could even begin to be found. While there were endless tales of them living all over the world, nothing of recent sightings reported them flying to any potential lair, even if they existed now at all.

Styrkar thanked Olavi for his information and paid him handsomely for his assistance. He then ordered Torill to come with him, for it was time to go. He would find the Blood of the Dead God and the black opal first, since their locations were known. They rode for the old Crystal Mountains, a four day ride from the Forest of Ever Night. The green mountains looked nothing like crystal and resembled the Grey Mountains of the South and the mountains of the Nordlands. Styrkar and Torill rode into one of the valleys and began traveling on the winding roads up the side of the mountains. Torill complained when she started to get cold from the altitude, but he ignored her. For several days, they rode up and down the mountains and Torill got very ill from it, but Styrkar refused to stop and rest, except during the night so the horses could sleep.

They had traversed the face of the tallest of the Crystal Mountains and noticed a trail going up the steep, sharp face. Scaling it, they found a narrow cave opening and crawled head first into it.

It was obvious, then, why these were the Crystal Mountains, for the entire interior was of the most flawless, clear crystal either Styrkar or Torill had ever seen. They vibrated and were warm with energy that flowed into and out of the visitors as they crawled along in the extremely narrow tunnel.

And then they saw it. Glowing an angry, evil scarlet in the mounting darkness were red crystals with malevolent dark spots within. It was the resting place of the Dead God Abbath when he escaped his brother's fury. Styrkar ordered Torill to go into the chamber, since she was thinner and smaller than he was, and retrieve a piece of the Blood. With a crude chisel and a hammer, she crawled ahead and could barely fit through the opening into the chamber. Once in, she looked at the Blood in awe, for the whole chamber glowed in red and strange thoughts entered her head. These thoughts told her that she could take that hammer and split Styrkar's skull and be long gone to another part of the world by the time he was even discovered. She looked deviously in his direction and was startled back to reality to see he already had his battleaxe in hand, as if he anticipated any attack. She quickly chipped off a significantly sized piece and handed it up to Styrkar. He then ordered her to return the hammer and chisel up to him before he would pull her out. She did so and he stuck them in his belt before grabbing her by her wrists and backing out of the narrow, crystal tunnel.

As they rode back down the mountain with the Blood of the Dead God with the bone of the damned in the saddle bag, they witnessed an odd site-one of the largest birds they had ever seen, black with a huge, wedge-like crest of crimson and cobalt upon the top of his head, skimmed along the surface of a mountain lake below. They watched in awe for a few minutes, as it would put its head in the water for fish and circle back once it reached one of the shores of the long lake.

They must have taken a different road out of the Crystal Mountains, for when they left, even though the landscape looked similar, they found a village at the base of the mountain. They rode in and found it abandoned, but as it was getting dark and the Witching Season began thundering its arrival with great strokes of blue lightning. They barely made it into the village and into one of the stone cottages there with the horses when the rain came down in droves. The roof leaked in spots, for the cottage had not been tended to and maintained for decades, but it kept most of the rain out and the two riders dry.

Torill had become seriously ill and shivered as she pulled her blankets around her in an effort to keep warm. Styrkar watched her with baleful, blue eyes from his corner. At first, he did nothing but let her suffer the nightmares and fever, but the Witches are known for their long visits, especially against mountains where clouds get anchored and can dump water gallon upon gallon for days. He gave her water and his blankets and laid next to her, holding her against him to keep her warm. This was the first of the Witches and it stayed for three days, keeping Styrkar and Torill trapped inside of the old cottage.

Torill awoke, still feeling queasy, to find Styrkar embracing her as he slept. The Witch hammered yet on the cottage and roared its fury through the ink black skies with no sign of relenting anytime soon. She went to push him away, and then changed her mind with an evil smirk as she noticed he had let his guard down and had forgotten to remove his weapon belt before laying with her to keep her warm. Gingerly, she took hold of the handle of his dagger with her fingertips and slowly drew it from its scabbard. Once the blade was totally clear, she brought it to her and with a quick thrust, drove it into his belly.

He jolted awake with a cry and she scrambled to try to escape from him. Styrkar grabbed her by her throat and flung her as hard as he could into one of the cold, stone walls before grabbing the dagger with both hands and forcibly tearing it out of himself. She stood up, but barely had time to dive out of his way when he lunged at her with the blood-drenched blade. The horses whinnied loudly, almost screaming, as she ran for the door, but even wounded, Styrkar was faster than she was and tackled her, both falling out into the torrential downpour. She managed to scurry out from underneath of him and he managed to get to his feet to chase her, but only managed to reel along for a few steps before collapsing to the ground and landing face down in the pouring rain. Torill stopped after some distance and realized he was not chasing her. Instead of running away, however, she crept back to see where he was, although she could not understand why she had to go look.

Styrkar was laying face down with his blood streaming out into the mud. She grinned, believing him dead, and ran to the cottage to get the horses, stepping carefully around his body. Torill climbed on her horse and tried to grab his, but found the beast would not come near her. Nevertheless, she rode off into the storm.

She would not get too far, for the small springs turn to streams during the Season of Witches and streams turn to raging rivers. The paths and roads were flooded to the point of being impassible. Torill was faced with risking her life trying to travel during a Witch, or to go back to the cottage where Styrkar lay dead and waterlogged. She decided upon the latter, but when she returned, the Son of Arnkell's body was not there. The rain was pouring down so violently that should could not make out tracks or blood trails leading anyplace.

Grabbing a soaked tree limb, she cautiously entered the cottage. Styrkar's horse was there and reared up, letting out what sounded like a high scream. She noticed mud and water and blood on the dirty, fungus-laden wood floor going in, but before she could react to what she had seen, Styrkar had her by her drowned hair and saturated slave rags and threw her into the floor in the corner, sending the branch skidding off to a dark corner. A lightning bolt lit up the sky with a blue light for a second and in that second, she saw him draw his long sword. She frantically begged and pleaded with him to not kill her and that she would never try such a thing again. He held the weapon to her face and told her that she would stitch the wound she had given him with his dagger and if she tried to fix it so he would bleed to death from it, she would fall ahead of him into the Abyss.

Torill was forbidden to lay down the remainder of their hiding from the Witch's fury. When the weather was finally clear two days later, Styrkar tied a rope to her and guided her as she walked behind his horse. By the time they reached a small town with its inn, he had calmed down considerably, but still would not allow her near him. He remained at the town until the priest there removed the stitches from the scar and the two were on their way to the Shadow Wood.

It had been the home of people similar to those of the Forbidden Lands and the Forest of Ever Night, but now it was empty of them and in its place were mostly bandits and rangers and trappers and anyone else who preferred the solitude of the great forest. Unlike the Forest of Ever Night, however, and the Spectre Wood, the sun did shine through ancient limbs to the forest floor and cast dark shadows, hence its name. Here and there were the remains of finely carved homes of the Children of the Forest, the predominantly blonde members of their kind. The trees here, too, were gingkoes of untold age, but mixed with oaks and maples and alders.

Styrkar had Torill climb every tree and search for the black opal orchid. This lasted for days and she nearly fell a couple of times from the giant trees, but after her little escape stunt in the cottage ruin, she was not eager to incur his wrath. She finally came upon the orchid nestled in a particularly high gingko tree and carefully removed it from its lofty home. Again, as she struggled to climb down the trunk, she felt her feet lose their hold and she plummeted for the forest floor. Styrkar caught her this time, for she had the flower he needed. He took the flower from her and wrapped it gently in a sack and placed it carefully in the saddlebag with the bone and the gem. The only thing that they needed now was the impossible one-the heart of the dragon.

Styrkar was at a loss on what to do, especially when he remembered when he last saw a dragon. It was in the Abyss and he was not eager to go there again any time soon. He thought some more. That body must be long gone after all that time anyway, he thought- decomposed or consumed or whatever happens to the dead in that unholy place. Then he remembered a good deal of his quests had been to ruined cities in deserts and he stroked his beard in deep thought about the Endless Wastes, pondering if ancient dragons could live in the desert.

The Shadow Wood, like the Spectre wood, had grew beyond its original borders over the centuries since the days Eroc roamed the world and wrote of strange things that no man before and no man since could ever know save through him. The forest now reached the ruins of the old merchant city of Carvannia, which by the descriptions from legends and tomes must have looked very similar to the cities of Aardsberg and Tuska with great domes and colorful minarets and towers reaching for the skies.

It had been a vast place by the amount of foundations and masonry left behind. Styrkar marveled that a city of its size had ever existed in those dark days of the fifth and sixth civilizations. Before long, they came upon the plaza of Carvannia, where the likeness of Eroc was said to exist. It was there, among the broken mosaics and paving stones with the grass and weeds and trees pushing past them and with four other effigies, mounted on a horse and charging into battle with his sword aloft. It had been crafted from marble that had stained and aged over the years, but the Witches were not as violent here as they were even mere miles to the north, so the statues were still very much intact. There were two smoothly hammered metal flumes for water, oddly without rust, with the whole thing representing some charge Eroc and his Bards were involved in-something greatly important but lost in the annals of time.

The Great Sage himself was unimpressive, if it was believed that the statues were life-sized. The figure on the horse was a mere five to five and a half feet tall if he were able to stand up, and he was not obese or sickly skinny like many sages Styrkar or Torill had seen. They suspected he was average, neither muscular nor bony, under the robes he wore. He had a draconic look about him, with a long, wide nose and narrow, sinister eyes. His hair had been long, longer than Styrkar had imagined and most of all, he looked human. It had been rumored in legends that he was either some kind of angel or a demon, but whatever it was, he was looked no different than the Children of Ice and of the Forest. As they stared at it, Styrkar decided to find a sage in the nearby port city that was built upon the western remains of the Carvannia. It was nothing impressive, for Tuska and Takros had taken the place of the old merchant city when it fell.

Once in the small city of Knoris, Styrkar sought out the sage there and asked him about dragons. The sage told him none existed, but unlike others, this sage sounded different. He hesitated before he answered that and his reply was thinly veiled. Styrkar mentioned the one in the Abyss and was told the Abyss had countless dragons, but none existed in this world. Styrkar then asked of Eroc and his burial place. Again, the sage hesitated and replied that the tomb was on the Isle of Nemh far below the sea. Styrkar asked of the statues and the sage actually answered it directly. They had been carved to commemorate Eroc and his siblings defeating the then dreaded Bastians when they invaded Carvannia. He also let slip that the last surviving Carvannians in the Sea of Mystics tended the statues, just as they had tended a temple to him, until the last one died several decades ago. Styrkar asked about the temple, but the sage said no temple existed. When confronted with his contradiction, he replied that he was wrong and reiterated that no temple existed and no dragons existed.

Seeing that this was going nowhere, Styrkar asked him about the Endless Wastes and the rumor that secret and ancient things were in the desert. The sage denied it, claiming there was only desert as far as the eye can see and as far as the soul can travel before the sands claim him. Finally, the Nordman left, but now knowing that a temple to Eroc existed somewhere. As he and Torill exited the hut, a cowled man whispered from the shadows and offered to tell them anything they wished to know, for he had been listening outside and knew the fat, old man would never give up the secrets of the Great Sage. He told them to follow him to his hut, which was a very tiny, one room hovel near the wharves. The thing barely looked like it could withstand even a mild breeze and had a low doorway and ceiling that forced the towering Styrkar to bow over before entering. Once seated at a crudely made table in crudely made chairs, the man informed them that the Temple of Eroc did indeed exist and it was not on the ill-fated Isle of Nemh, but in a place the Carvannians knew it would be safe from those who desecrate and rob graves-in the Endless Wastes. Far into the Endless Wastes, near those places that were sacred to both contemporary men and to those of old civilizations. Styrkar had found one when he went to the hiding place of the orb a few years before. The hooded man told them, too, that in the days of Eroc, there were dragons-many dragons. In Eroc's tomb was said to be his serpent Blackwyrd, for Eroc's mount was a dragon. In more obscure legends spoken in these parts, the Great Sage was also a great wizard and was considered by the Carvannians to be the most powerful warlock in all of Terrascape in that day. It was not recommended, however, to attempt to take on Blackwyrd, he warned in whispers, although he did not elaborate as to why.

Eroc's death had been a cause of great mourning and the Carvannians buried him, his three Bards-Torg, Ildjarn and Thorkell-and his sisters and brother each in separate tombs in a cave deep within the Endless Wastes. Where the tombs were, however, he could not say, for there are many secrets in the Endless Wastes and the desert keeps its secrets well hidden.

Then he spoke of dragons. It was said that when the Isle of Nemh sunk into the Sea of Mystics, the dragons flew into the desert, where they became guardians of what lay there. Any of the ancient sites may be home to one of more of those creatures, so to find a dragon, one only need to find any one of the secrets of the Endless Wastes.

Styrkar and Torill were warned again in hushed tones, though, that whatever they found in the forbidding sands must stay there, for men were not meant to learn every secret of the past and some secrets were better left undiscovered and unknown.

The next day, Styrkar arranged for a messenger to take back to Tuska the bone of the damned soul, the Blood of the Dead God and the black opal so the desert sands and the desert heat would not harm them. Once he and Torill had gathered together their supplies, they rode south into the region where the Grey Mountains met the Crystal Mountains and that separated the barren sands from the fertile Northern lands. The journey was mostly uneventful, save riding past the occasional ruin or cemetery. After passing the first of the mountains, the Witches no longer threatened them and the sky was mostly clear with exception to the nights and early morning hours when fog filled the valleys and ravines. Torill and Styrkar kept their distance from each other for the entire ride through the mountains, speaking very little unless necessity ordered them to do so. Seven days later, they crossed the knobs of red rock that were the beginning of the Fingers of Blood and into the sun-bleached sands of the Endless Wastes beyond.

Even though they covered their heads with their blankets, Torill was not used to the dry, oppressive heat and was nauseous by the afternoon of the first day. Styrkar refused to stop for her to rest and she muttered curses at him for it. They slept apart from each other on the warm sand when night fell, hoping that some desert beast would devour the other loudly enough so they could wake up and escape safely. When the morning sun peered over the horizon, they both were disappointed to see the other still alive.

They still did not speak to each other beyond necessity as they rode further into the glaring sands, but Styrkar stuttered to himself the various stories his mother had told him of the Endless Wastes and Torill found herself listening to him with interest. Around noon, they spotted towers in the distance and first believed it to be tricks played upon them by the heat, for Styrkar knew he was nowhere near Al-Zar. But as they drew closer, it became clear it was no mirage. There was a city that looked like the ancient basalt ruins-every building, every dome and every tower was a dull black and lacking the elaborate, painstakingly carved ornamentation of Al-Zar. This was Al-Amon.

When they entered the gates of the city, angry eyes from women shrouded in burqas and men wrapped in shemaghs fell upon Torill, even though she was mostly covered with the blanket. Styrkar stopped at a merchant's awning and bought his slave a burqa to cover all but her blue eyes and himself a shamagh to hide his long, blonde hair and goatee so he would not look out of place, although he was far taller than most of the natives of Al-Amon. They stayed there for two days, during which time they inquired about dragons, but the xenophobic denizens refused to answer except to mutter about Abu.

Torill and Styrkar were more than happy to leave Al-Amon and welcomed the inhospitable desert with its sands harshly reflecting the sun and heat. They were two hour's ride from the city, still wearing their shrouds and not talking to each other, when they heard a voice call from behind, at first faint, but growing closer each time it beckoned. It was the nasal voice of an Abuist man on a white Jharkan steed. They turned their horses around and Styrkar drew his battleaxe to confront him. The man waved and called out that he came in peace and had overheard them asking about dragons. He introduced himself as Ahmad and that he was a nomad who had knowledge of the location of the Place of Dragons. If the two pagan infidels wished any chance of finding it, they needed a guide such as himself. Styrkar accepted his offer and the man rode next to him, talking about the people of Al-Amon and his tribe, which both northerners gathered he had been cast out of by his use of the past tense.

After a while, Ahmad finally spoke of the Place of Dragons. Legend had it that when the last of the Children of Lamna, the people from which came the Great Sage Eroc, passed away, the Dragons came into the desert and nested among the ruins and secret places there. Many nested not far from the Tombs of Darksinger, where the surviving Carvannians hid the bodies of Eroc and his Bards so that none could find them. Ahmad, however, had found them-great cliffs of red rock in the middle of nowhere where great black serpents soar and nest. He said that without someone who knew the desert, they were impossible to find, just as most everything else held secret deep in the Endless Wastes. He also managed to convince the two that they needed to ride at night to avoid the torture of the sun.

He mentioned at times the other secrets in his conversations over the next few days-of that place that was where man came into the world and that something mysterious and evil literally hung in the sky there, of a place of great pyramids that rivaled those found in the sands of the Abyss, of tombs which changed in the blink of an eye, of the remains of great floating cities that plummeted from the skies and of other such places scattered about the sands that went on forever. He said the last of the Children of Lamna, Per, had seen what lurks upon the other side, although nothing was written of what he had found there nor was anything mentioned in the oral legends about the lands beyond the Endless

Wastes. At one point during their journey in the desert, Styrkar and Torill thought they

saw something in the distant twilight sky that hovered and looked like no bird, but it was

too far for them to be certain and Ahmad had seen fit to guide them away from it.

  They traveled over a week and a half before the first sign they were near the Place of

Dragons appeared-a great, dark serpent was flying, silhouetted by the setting desert sun.

It was larger than the half fiend dragon that Styrkar fought in the Abyss and paid no

attention to the small humans running around on horses and mules in the sand. In another

two days, they arrived at the blood red cliffs upon which many dragons perched and some

flew around. Caves dotted the rocky face and not far from the sudden jagged peak were

the ruins of a small village, the foundations and walls betraying that it was of Carvannian

origin. Even more surprising was from one solitary bleached house rose puffs of smoke

from a fire and within the open windows was the warm glow of a fireplace and candle

light.

  Ahmad knocked upon the dry, grey door of the place and from within was heard a

shuffling and a hoarse, gentle voice of a man called out that he was coming. The door

creaked open and there stood the hunched, skeletal form of a man with long white hair.

He welcomed them to his humble home and confirmed to Ahmad that he was indeed a

descendant of the Carvannians who had brought the remains of Eroc and his Bards to the

Endless Wastes to protect them from the civilization that was rising from a place called

Rhedia. That name was familiar to Styrkar, for it was said that the people of Murtha were

descendants of the Rhedians, which the man could neither conform nor deny. Their host

asked them why they had come and Styrkar explained his need for the heart of a dragon so he could have weapons powerful enough to kill the king of Stromgald, who had killed his family. The man smiled weakly and told him that he was welcomed to take the heart of any dragon except for that of the Scythe Dragons, especially the ancient wyrm Blackwyrd, who diligently guarded the tomb and temple of Eroc, his rider in life. He then asked his three guests to accompany him to the temple that night so they could pray to Styrkar's success in his quest of vengeance.

This surprised Torill and Styrkar, for most priests save those of Abu spoke harshly of revenge, but the host explained to them that Eroc himself had quested for revenge and such a cause should have the Great Sage's blessing. When Ahmad spoke of false gods, the man explained that when the Dead God had finally been put to death, despite what those who still followed him believed, Eroc took his place in the heavens as the Lord of the Stars, for Eroc was the most powerful of all of his kind and dwelled still among the constellations with his allies, even if his mortal body remained in a tomb in the middle of the Gods' sandbox.

So after having a meal of flat bread and goat cheese, the man, who revealed his name to be Hawklorn, although he confessed to being merely a descendant of the legendary Carvannian, took them to the cliffs with a torch in hand and amid a chorus of dragon songs to an opening with protrusions and an overhang that looked like a dragon's head and into a chamber with five gates. A basalt stele outside each gate announced in the ancient runes of the Children of Lamna the occupants of each tomb and Hawklorn translated them. One tomb was that of Eroc's eldest sister Nebel, although not much was known of her. One tomb was of the sister Runesong and her mate Krakhas, both of whom were great warriors. Runesong, however, died during childbirth and Krakhas millennia later, for all of the Children of that time-of Ice, of Forest and of Lamna-lived long lives, longer than any human could fathom. One tomb was that of Gorsedd, one of Eroc's brothers, who was in his own right a god-the Lord of the Seas, although his temples were only in the remotest of seaside towns since the fall of Carvannia. One tomb was that of the three Bards of Azatoth-Ildjarn, Torg and Thorkell-who served Eroc faithfully and who wrote the fifth, sixth and seventh books of a faith that would die with Hawklorn. Torg was Eroc's youngest brother and Thorkell was one of his cousins. The final tomb was the tomb and temple of Eroc, the Midnight Angel, and the very stone to it had worn in it a wide groove from the many feet of worshippers during the final days of the old kingdoms. It was to this tomb that he guided them.

The grate here was unlocked and Hawklorn entered it cautiously. A great sighing over a soft hum could be heard within and fire could be seen burning in the braziers ahead. They entered the chamber and found out it was not sighing, but breathing, for to their left was the largest dragon they had yet seen. Blackwyrd was a beautiful winged beast of swirly violet, indigo and black and with a pair of long ivory horns. He gazed upon them with aged eyes that glowed an ultraviolet purple, but he made no move at them. The ceilings were covered in a mosaic of lapis lazuli and fire opals and depicted the stars of all the heavens and in the center of the room was the whirring and spinning astrolabe Hawklorn said had been taken from Eroc's chambers on the doomed Nemh and placed in the tomb, where it still functioned and kept track of the planets of the system and their moons. Eroc's sarcophagus sat in front of the astrolabe and upon it was graven his image, holding his sword in death and his eyes closed in eternal sleep. And in front of that was the fossil stone altar with elaborate carvings of dragons upon it.

Hawklorn told his guests to kneel before the altar to receive Eroc's blessing on the quest, but Ahmad refused, calling it a blasphemy and an affront, but he quieted down when the great wyrm growled deeply, as if Blackwyrd understood every word the Abuist was uttering. The host prayed to Eroc and, as he invoked the name of the Great Sage, there was an indigo glow that started on the altar and jumped to Styrkar and Torill. Then an image appeared over the altar of a great blue dragon. This was the one, Hawklorn said, that Eroc chose for them to have and that they should find this dragon after having a good rest.

The three visitors slept in Hawklorn's home and the next night, Styrkar and Torill set out to find the dragon they were told to kill. They scaled the steep red cliffs to reach the top of the Place of Dragons and there, resting upon an overhang, was the blue dragon they sought. Styrkar attacked the beast and it retaliated with long strokes of lightning, for despite what Eroc and Styrkar had wanted, it was not eager to become a part of someone's sword and battleaxe. The shock of the breath attack knocked the Nordman down and stunned him. The dragon swept him with his tail, stirring up red dust and nearly flipping Styrkar off of the cliff, much to Torill's amusement. The Son of Arnkell managed to hang on to his weapons, though, and hopped up on the balls of his feet and again rushed the big, blue serpent, which reared up and let loose another stroke of lightning, but Styrkar avoided it this time and was able to impale the beast's tail with his long sword. The dragon roared in pain and began snapping his tail around, finally flinging his tormentor into a massive boulder, sending his weapons spinning to the ground.

Styrkar slumped, the wind knocked out of him and in pain. Torill smirked, but was herself forced to dive for cover when the beast turned his attention to her and tried to rake her with his great claws. She scrambled for her master's long sword, which had landed closest to her, and tumbled under the dragon. As he reared again, Torill lunged and caught the dragon in his belly. Angrily, she twisted the sword and he howled an ungodly howl. She stabbed him violently several more times, spraying blood all over her burqa. The dragon stiffened up, then toppled over with a crash. Muttering curses at her Fantoftian master, she slashed open the dragon's chest with the sword and carefully cut out the heart.

Styrkar was just getting on his feet when Torill strode over haughtily and placed the huge, dripping heart before him and declared the dragon dead. As he took his sword back, she asked him if she could make some armor from the dragon's skin. He told her to find his axe and bring it to him. She sighed and looked for the weapon with her teeth grinding. Styrkar did let her take enough blue dragon skin to make armor after she had returned with the battleaxe, however, and put the still beating heart into a sack and fixed it upon his saddle. With his battleaxe, he lopped off the beast's head and Hawklorn took him back into the sanctuary of Eroc so he could place the head as an offering before the altar, for it was too big to place it upon the altar itself.

The next night, an injured Styrkar, with his slave and his guide, bid Hawklorn a farewell and left for Al-Amon and from there, home. The ride to Al-Amon was uneventful, but the earlier inquiries by Styrkar and Torill had attracted the attention of the Abuists who had tailed Styrkar and Kaisa years earlier, for none who follow the teachings of Abu have short memories and especially not forgiving natures. They sought out the infidel who questioned for those things that should be forbidden to all men for their blasphemous nature, and plotted his murder. As he stayed in an inn in Al-Amon to heal from his injuries, five men crept up to his room-four to grab him by his arms and legs and one to slit his throat, for they figured he would put up a fight.

Torill heard their hushed voices as they came up the stairs and woke Styrkar up from his slumber. The two quickly took up weapons-him the battleaxe and her the sword-and waited for them to enter the room. The door opened with a low creak and as the first man stuck his head in to see where the Nordman and his slave girl were, Styrkar liberated him of it with one great cleave. He fell, blood spilling from his open neck. The other four ran, screaming in the language of the desert folk. After that, none came to kill him again.

Styrkar traveled three days later, feeling very ill yet but not eager to have himself killed before he had a chance to mete out his revenge on Aethelwulf. They were happy to be rid of Al-Amon and welcomed the site of the Blood Fingers and the mountains beyond. Again, the journey through the mountains was uneventful and they fell into the foothills beyond during the onset of one of the Witches. They did not stop to rest until reaching the lowly cottages and shanties of Knoris, where they rode out the rest of the week long storm.

As they passed through the Shadow Wood on their way home, still avoiding conversation with one another, Aethelwulf broke his truces and attacked the new city of Styrkarskog in the Northern kingdoms. The Horsemen there fought valiantly against the king's armies, but this time, he had a much better general-Baldwin. After five days, the city fell and Thorbjorn was captured and ceremoniously murdered by Baldwin. Those Horsemen not killed fled into the wilderness and into the Spectre Wood. A regiment followed them, but as the soldiers in it were from the other side of the continent and ignorant of the regions and legends of these lands, they were caught in the Woods by a horror, possibly the one Torill and Styrkar had avoided by luck during their visit, and their bones joined those of the damned on the forest floor.

News of Aethelwulf's treaty breaking and the fall of Styrkarskog spread quickly and reached the ears of Styrkar and Torill as they left the Forest of Ever Night and they spurred their horses on for Tuska. The Son of Arnkell felt an urgency to get his weapons enchanted now, for the time was right for him to hunt down the dreaded king. They stopped long enough to rest the horses and arrived in Tuska sooner than expected.

The city was in a commotion. Refugees of Styrkarskog had flooded the streets, for again, Aardsberg refused them entry, and the militia there had their hands full with both preparing for the inevitability that Aethelwulf would come and the onslaught of refugees. Styrkar and Torill finally arrived at the warlock's home and gave the heart of the dragon to him to at last enchant Styrkar's weapons so he could kill Aethelwulf.

The process took an hour and involved some bizarre rituals and spell casting that Styrkar was not interested in learning the meanings of. Astrid had warned him about the dangers of becoming involved in the matters of magicians and he had taken that advice, for the most part, into consideration. When finished, the sword and the battleaxe both burned with a blue flame and bore the cryptic runes of their enchantments upon their blades and handles. The wizard did not hand them to Styrkar, however-he told the Nordman to pick up the weapons himself. Upon laying his hands on them, he was hit with a vision of Aethelwulf and Baldwin riding behind their armies along a well-traveled road that he knew was a road to Aardsberg.

The wizard explained the visions to him-whoever was Styrkar's enemy, these weapons would show Styrkar where that enemy was at all times. They also could cut cleanly and any injured by them would continue bleeding until dead or someone tended to the wound. There was also a chance that anyone hit by these weapons would turn to stone. They never needed sharpening and the blue flame could serve to illuminate the dark, even in close places, for the blue fire did not burn nor give off smoke. The wizard, too, was sure the weapons could do more, but was not sure of what those effects could be. Styrkar returned home and fetched the money to pay him handsomely, returning to do so himself. Then Torill asked the wizard, after her master went back to his apartment to rest and tend to his wolves, to make her armor from the blue dragon hides. Knowing she could not pay, the wizard said that he would do so if she fulfilled a quest for him. She agreed to do it and he told her what he wanted.

He told her that ages ago, the Spectre Wood was a scene of a great battle between the worldly forces that worshipped a god and an arch devil. Because of this battle and the nature of magic used, the forest had strange properties. He told her of two rumors. The first was of a swamp not far from the coast where it was said the bodies of warriors lay in stasis under its brackish waters. One of the bodies, however, is that of a great mage who owned a staff made of a rare wood and that held great power. If what he had heard of the ability of the waters there to preserve things as they had been were true, the staff would still be there and waiting to be freed from the ghoulish tomb of its master. The other was of a city below the waters of the Sea of Mystics that had somehow been involved in the battle there as well and it was said that a magical ring existed in that city. It was heavily guarded by things he could not describe, for those who had seen them were never sane enough to do so afterward, and he gave her a long sword that he had created for a time when he could break away from his services for Kjell or when someone powerful enough came to him who could go to the ruins under the sea. He told her that it was effective best against creatures that dwelled in the deep sea. Then, from a small wooden box, he removed several metal vials and told her that the potion within would allow her to breathe underwater. His final item for her was a note to Styrkar and Kjell, requesting for Torill to carry out an errand of dire importance to him, both of which reluctantly granted be carried out.

Torill used the mule Styrkar had acquired for her and headed for the Spectre Wood. She was not enthralled about being anywhere near the Spectre Wood, let alone any of its marshes. She rode along just outside of the fen's boundaries for a place to camp so she could be near it without having to actually sleep in that evil place. She found a spot and since there were a few hours of daylight left, she searched in areas closest to her tent, but found nothing. The next morning, she reluctantly ventured further into the swamp. For over a mile, there was nothing but brackish, smelly water and mud covered in green slime among dead and blackened trees.

And then she saw the first one. It was staring up with irisless eyes, widened in permanent horror, from just below the surface of the stinking water and was of a bearded man, pale and bloated in his steel armor. He was where he had fallen countless years ago, preserved by whatever unholy quality this swamp possessed. She spotted two more near him, another warrior face down and a man who, by his elaborately embroidered tunic, was a cleric of some sort to a god she could not identify readily. As she walked, she saw more and more, some alone and others in groups or stacked on top of each other, some in shallow pools and others so deep as to barely be visible. At one group of dead, bloated

warriors, she spotted a faint red glow of something long buried mostly in the murk. She

reached into the cursed waters and pulled out a long sword that spoke in her mind thanks

for being found. She gleefully ran back to camp and spent the rest of the day cleaning the

scum and sludge from it and drying it off with rags from Styrkar's house.

At dusk, she went back into the swamp of the dead and searched for the staff the warlock

in Tuska had requested. She had her newfound sword with her and it told her that there

had been a contingent of war wizards that had been killed in this battle and the location of

where those wizards had fallen. Torill followed its directions and found several bodies,

some of creatures she did not recognize and could not be from this planet or plane and

some of humans or Children. From the base of a nearby dead tree, she saw a bright blue

light from something tangled in the vines. After fighting with it for several minutes, she

pulled it free and saw she had found a great black staff that looked as if it had been

crafted from one of the dead trees' roots. Clutched by wood talons at the top of the staff

was a crystal and within the crystal was a blue and red vortex. The sword spoke into her

mind again, congratulating her on finding the staff.

Torill took the sword and staff with her as she rode for where the marshes met the sea

and where the city rested inundated. As she rode, the sword told her of the battle. He

claimed he was a warrior who had been killed and his soul was sucked into his weapon

and trapped in a pool of algae-infested water of an unwholesome nature. He was part of

the armies of Abbath, known as the Dead God, and had been killed trying to destroy the

armies of Darfos in the arch devil's power play. He did not recall the exact spells used to

cause the city to be flooded, the swamp cursed or the forest haunted, although he guessed that there was a divine hand in the matter. Instead of either side winning and gaining the favor of the lords they served, they were deceived and forced to haunt the forest, remain unburied and watch their bodies decompose in the forest or be waterlogged for eternity. He told her the city was much the same-preserved in the state it was in when the battle had occurred and that whatever terrors had been unleashed by the warlocks and demons still lived there, even under the surface of the water.

The iron gates leading into the city still stood visible above the water in low tide and no coral grew upon them, no algae stained them and no barnacles or bivalves anchored themselves to it. They had been damaged long ago during the battle, but time had inflicted no other effect upon them. The walls stretched out and sunk below the waters of the angry sea. Torill left her new sword on her mule and took up the sword the warlock had given her. As she followed the soggy, peat path leading into the gates and the water beyond it, she drank the first vial she would need to complete her quest. She waded in further and the water closed in over her head, but whatever that potion was, she found herself able to breathe underwater. She passed farmhouses that had supplied the city with food when it was of the world above and entered another set of metal gates. She was not sure how far down she was, but the city was beautiful, with large towers and elaborate gables and eaves of an architecture that spoke of a time too long ago for her to fathom. There were more people here, in the buildings and in a similar state as their counterparts in the swamp.

Then she spotted something that froze her blood. A bloated body, although she was not sure if it was one of the preserved dead or some hapless sailor, was half eaten by something and was stuck through a broken window. She came upon another and another and she realized that something or some things that had a taste for human or human-like flesh lived here. She searched each house and each hand she found, stopping to drink from two more vials in air pockets within the sunken buildings.

When she entered one small building, she saw the beast that was eating the dead-an amorphous abomination made up of gibbering mouths and flailing tentacles-and she swam away as fast as she could with a sword in her hand, her mind racing and threatening to snap. It had spotted her and came after her, propelling itself with a long, eel-like tail. Torill knew she could not outrun it, but was hoping to lure it to a place where she could kill it easily and without sustaining much harm, especially since all she had were still the rags given to her by Kjell's captains who had captured her. She managed to barely make it into a narrow alleyway and the slavering horror tried to push itself through, but Torill launched herself into an attack on it with the sword, killing the beast in a few well-placed strokes. She carved open the beast's belly in hopes that the ring she sought would be there, but all she could find were partly digested body parts, fragments of armor and broken furniture and a sword made useless by the stomach acids. She sighed and continued her search.

She finally happened upon the ring in a dark house that sat far from the rest of the city. It was far enough out that she had not noticed it at first, but when she rose to the surface to drink another potion, she saw it. It sat along a road that ran out of the north gates and on a hill. Torill felt that before fooling with the city any further, she must go investigate that house. There was no sign of who lived there or what the house was for, for it was completely empty, but from under a floorboard in the house was a glow of sinister violet and Torill pried them loose with her sword to find the ring there, having fallen off of its master's finger and into a knot hole in the wood of the floor.

Torill made haste to get to the surface and swim for the nearest land, for she had seen something else when she spotted the house during her earlier surfacing-more insidious beasts that she was loathe to describe to anyone-and she was not eager to overplay her good fortune of having been able to kill one. Once on land, she rode to a place a safe distance for her to camp, away from any of those insidious beasts or damned souls or whatever else lurked the Spectre Wood, before riding for Tuska the next morning with the quested items and her new sword.

Styrkar had left for Aardsberg when she returned with the staff and ring. Torill made a bee line for the warlock's home and, still weary from her ordeal, returned the sword he had given her, as well as giving him the items he requested. He thanked her and returned with her armor from the blue dragon's hide. However, he told her she would have to wait until Styrkar returned in order to receive it, for he had to give her permission to have it. She argued that since he had given her the hide, he had, in essence, given her permission. The wizard refused to budge on the matter, insisting that she must go through Lord Kjell or, better yet, Styrkar in order for him to give it to her. Finally able to argue no more, she lunged at him, knocking him down to the floor, and stabbed him with his dagger repeatedly and in such anger that his blood flung onto the walls and ceiling. She took her armor and the staff and ring she had recovered and used the candles from his study to set his home on fire.

Torill returned to Styrkar's apartment long enough to change her rags for one of his Nordlander tunics and a pair of his pants before fleeing for the gates. Upon seeing the guards running around and the commotion of the tower fire and the murder of the wizard who served Lord Kjell, she made haste for the nearest entrance to the sewers and from there, found her way through pits of raw sewage and vile water out of Tuska.

Styrkar had arrived in Aardsberg with his pack of wolves a day or two after Aethelwulf had begun his siege of the city. Fire was raging through those sections outside the city walls and the camp of the refugees of places already destroyed by the Stromgald army as screams and cries of battle and of the dying echoed across the valleys. This was of no concern to him, however. He was interested in only one person and one alone-Aethelwulf. He knew the dreaded king was here, for he had seen him in the visions from the weapons the warlock of Tuska had crafted for him. Styrkar spurred his horse on and charged into battle.

He was greeted with a small unit of soldiers from the far reaches of the continent, in places far from the Nordlands, the Sea of Mystics and the Endless Wastes. They fell upon him in an attempt to overwhelm him, but the wolves of Hazor, now numbering over twenty, tore the foreign soldiers from limb to limb. They then ran before the Houndmaster as he drove further into the battle, attacking and rending to pieces all who tried to interfere with him as he searched the field for Aethelwulf. Those who managed to avoid the wolves were hacked apart by Styrkar's battleaxe, some screaming in agony as their flesh and blood turned into stone.

He was eventually spotted by Baldwin on the battlefield. The blackguard gathered together his knights, other blackguards who were sought out and recruited by the former leader of the Blue Tygers, and rode out to meet him. When Baldwin ordered a charge, Styrkar ordered his wolves to attack. The blackguards who were no strangers to the legends of the wolves of Hazor fled, for they had no desire to be fed upon. The ones who did not, mostly those of the foreign stock Styrkar and his wolves had confronted earlier, fell victim to the icy breath of the beasts from Hazor and were frozen solid and were shattered and eaten.

Styrkar took on Baldwin himself. The two charged at one another with swords out and met with a clash of metal and the roaring whinnies of their mounts. They pounded hard enough on each other's shields and helmets that it was deafening, but when Baldwin made contact with Styrkar's reddish brown studded hellhound armor, there was a flare of fire that caused the knight to scream in agony as his eyes were burned out of the sockets. As the blackguard crawled around blindly for his sword, the Horseman jumped off of his horse and ripped the helmet from him and cleaved down upon his head as hard as he could, sending brains and blood splashing and turning Baldwin to stone. The Son of Arnkell collected up the dead knight's sword as a trophy and gave Aesir and the Blue Tygers control of his wolves until such a time he returned so that they could assist in the defense of the city and so that Styrkar could confront Aethelwulf alone.

It took him the better part of an evening and a day as he skulked about the vast battlefield, lurking and avoiding battle with anybody else, to find the King of Stromgald. He was not leading his troops this time, for the king's health had deteriorated considerably in the past five years and he was relying upon magical means even now to keep himself able to command his armies. He was camped in a tent behind far behind the battle and had his elite guard around him. Nevertheless, Styrkar let out a battle cry and descended upon the encampment. Seven burly warriors stood in his path and engaged him in battle, knocking him from his horse and attempting to overwhelm him, but

Styrkar's weapons caused two of them to die in screaming agony as they turned into stone and allowed two others to bleed to death from minor gashes as they clashed weapons with him. One fled into the wilderness. The other two he killed outright, for they would not run despite their comrades' horrific deaths.

Aethelwulf did not wait for him and had cast a spell that gated him away from Styrkar and the entire battle. Desperately, the Nordman used his weapons to see where his foe had fled and an image of the destroyed portal appeared in his mind's eye-Aethelwulf had escaped into the Spectre Wood. Styrkar threw his battleaxe down and swore angrily, then picked it up again, found his horse and rode for the haunted forest.

As he was leaving the battlefield, more of the enemy army attempted to engage him and were quickly dispatched by his axe. It was three hours later when he was finally clear of the invasion and on his way to kill Aethelwulf.

Aethelwulf had gated to the Spectre Wood in hopes of activating the portal and summoning a demonic hero to take on Styrkar, for he had learned through sages the existence of the portal and realized that he and his mages had initially misinterpreted the writings of the Great Sage Eroc. Unfortunately, he was not aware that Styrkar had destroyed the portal with a siege machine from the Abyss years before and he punched one of the stones and cursed, swearing to kill the Son of Arnkell. He noticed the fog starting to roll in and decided that perhaps for now, however, he should find shelter from those spirits and horrors that haunt the Spectre Wood before any of them had found him. He could hear the voices whispering to him and see the shadows fleeting among the trees and he was grateful to find one of the remains of the basalt towers, where he hid until the morning drove away that evil fog.

Torill had also returned to the Spectre Wood, albeit reluctantly. She did not know why, but something had told her to come here, for Kjell would never come into the haunted forest to find her. She hid during the nights when the fog rolled in and the souls of the damned fought each other and when that unspeakable horror lurked and stalked, slathering and hissing. When she rode during the day, the voices still whispered to her and the shadows followed her and she surely believed she would go mad if she had to stay in this unholy place for too long.

Both Torill and Aethelwulf had been hiding within the forest for days when Styrkar finally came to call. The Houndmaster made a beeline to the portal, but found that Aethelwulf was not there. He held the battleaxe in his hands and tried to focus on the king's location, ignoring the voices whispering his name at first. He could only see a dark tower, but he could not figure where in the Spectre Wood it was. Then he had an idea and answered the voices. After his ignoring them for so long every time he rode in, they were surprised when he suddenly acknowledged their calls. They told him that they sought redemption, for they no longer wanted to suffer in the Abyss during the day and haunt the forest at night. Styrkar asked them how he could free them. They told him that they did not know, but that if aiding him would help do so, then that was what they would do, for their damnation was for destroying the Great Trees and for unleashing the fiends of the Abyss into the sacred cities. They had hoped restoration of the Trees would absolve them, but that did not happen when Styrkar planted the seeds. They had hoped the destruction of the portal they had found would absolve them, but that did not happen when Styrkar destroyed it. Yet they were desperate to do something that might alleviate their suffering. Styrkar then asked them where King Aethelwulf was hiding. The souls did not know who

Aethelwulf was, but informed him that two entities had been lurking the forest, both

mortals. One was a man who was hiding in one of the basalt towers north of the portal.

The other was a girl who was riding around and sleeping among the ruins. They offered

to take him to both.

Styrkar requested only the one-the man. The souls, having been given a solace from the

condemnation of reenacting their battles for this night, took his warhorse by the reins. At

first, the beast reared and pulled away, but Styrkar nudged it with his knees and the

animal followed the guiding souls through the fog to the basalt tower ruins where the

sickly, evil king hid within.

They did not go there unnoticed, for Torill happened to be looking for shelter when she

noticed the ghosts of the wood guiding him and, against her instincts to hide, she

followed her former master, being certain to keep distance enough so as not to be spotted

by him.

The damned souls brought his horse before the ruins where Aethelwulf hid inside.

Styrkar jumped down from his horse with both weapons out, one in each hand, and strode

in to confront, finally, the man behind the deaths of his parents.

The king was huddled near his campfire, wheezing and hacking. He told Styrkar that the

dampness of the fog was playing havoc on his lungs. Then his sickly eyes fell upon his

visitor and he jolted to his feet, drawing his sword and balancing himself with one hand

on the devilishly carved walls. Styrkar introduced himself as the Son of Arnkell and

lunged at Aethelwulf. The king jumped out of his way and swung his blade at Styrkar's

head, but it rang as it hit the wall. The Horseman cleaved at Aethelwulf and nearly took

off his arm. Switching hands, the two continued to go at it, metal clanging and ringing as the two slashed and hacked at each other. The king snarled out an incantation and blinded Styrkar permanently with magic, but did not count on him knowing how to fight in total darkness. Aethelwulf stabbed at his foe, but when the tip made contact with the armor, a huge flash of fire sprayed forth, blinding the king and sending him scrambling on the ground for a hiding place, sputtering curses at Styrkar. He uttered another spell, but Styrkar struck out at him, lopping off the top of his head and spattering blood on the walls. But even with his brain exposed and mortally wounded, Aethelwulf insisted upon not dying. He sputtered at his adversary for interrupting his spell and dragged himself towards him. Styrkar asked him where the others were who had been involved in the attack on his village. Aethelwulf gasped loudly and told him that he had had them put to death, for not killing him all those years ago. He started another incantation, wheezing and croaking out the words, but the Horseman stabbed him again and there was a rasping cry as Aethelwulf was turned to stone and his soul was bound for all eternity to suffer in the Abyss by day and to haunt the woods at night, forever reenacting his death, along with all others who served devils and demons in a great battle that happened many millennia ago, for even aiding Styrkar against one of Baat'zaar's minions would not free their souls.

Styrkar felt a rush and dropped to his knees, drained finally of the anger he had felt for most of his adult life. Feeling his belt, he found the loop for his battleaxe and he slid it in with his hand, covered in blood from a shoulder wound inflicted upon him. He could not recall if he had gotten it from Baldwin or Aethelwulf or someone else. He stood on his feet and sheathed his sword before he began feeling his way to the door.

He did not know that outside that door, Torill was waiting. She had overheard the battle and knew the winner would eventually exit that tower ruin. And she knew from the death throes that she had heard that it would be Styrkar. As he stepped beyond the threshold with his arms outstretched to feel for his horse, she drove in as hard as she could with the sword that she had retrieved from that swamp of the dead.

The death of Styrkar was swift. Torill's sword had pierced his chest, impaling his lungs to his heart. A bright light filled his eyes and he could feel himself falling, sinking in slow motion. The sounds of the eternal battle of the damned-the echoes of clanging metal and the screams and cries of men long since dead-faded into eternal silence. He was content now, having avenged his parents' deaths only moments before, and his soul began its spiraling journey to Valhalla, place of the great warriors where he would fight for eternity by Kaisa and Arnkell's sides. He heard a voice with no sound, neither man nor woman nor of any creature known to him.

"Styrkar-you are not ready yet! There is still much to do!"

www.ingramcontent.com/pod-product-compliance
Lightning Source LLC
Chambersburg PA
CBHW020342260626
47156CB00004B/1650